TROUBLE ON THE TRAIL

Dag saw the silhouette of a man rise up from the ground, holding a rifle in his hands. The man brought the rifle up to his shoulder.

"Horton," Dag yelled.

Horton turned in surprise and swung his rifle toward Dag.

"Drop it," Dag yelled.

The man fired straight at Dag, without hesitation. Dag ducked even more and heard the bullet sizzle the air like an angry hornet.

Dag lined up the rear buckhorn sight with the front blade sight and squeezed the trigger. The butt of his rifle bucked against his shoulder. . . .

Ralph Compton

The Palo Duro Trail

A Ralph Compton Novel
by Jory Sherman

A SIGNET BOOK

SIGNET
Published by New American Library, a division of
Penguin Group (USA) Inc., 375 Hudson Street,
New York, New York 10014, USA
Penguin Group (Canada), 10 Alcorn Avenue, Toronto,
Ontario M4V 3B2, Canada (a division of Pearson Penguin Canada Inc.)
Penguin Books Ltd., 80 Strand, London WC2R 0RL, England
Penguin Ireland, 25 St. Stephen's Green, Dublin 2,
Ireland (a division of Penguin Books Ltd.)
Penguin Group (Australia), 250 Camberwell Road, Camberwell, Victoria 3124,
Australia (a division of Pearson Australia Group Pty. Ltd.)
Penguin Books India Pvt. Ltd., 11 Community Centre, Panchsheel Park,
New Delhi - 110 017, India
Penguin Group (NZ), Cnr Airborne and Rosedale Roads, Albany,
Auckland 1310, New Zealand (a division of Pearson New Zealand Ltd.)
Penguin Books (South Africa) (Pty.) Ltd., 24 Sturdee Avenue,
Rosebank, Johannesburg 2196, South Africa

Penguin Books Ltd., Registered Offices:
80 Strand, London WC2R 0RL, England

First published by Signet, an imprint of New American Library,
a division of Penguin Group (USA) Inc.

First Printing, December 2004
10 9 8 7 6 5 4 3 2 1

Printed in the United States of America

PUBLISHER'S NOTE
This is a work of fiction. Names, characters, places, and incidents either are
the product of the author's imagination or are used fictitiously, and any
resemblance to actual persons, living or dead, business establishments,
events, or locales is entirely coincidental.

THE IMMORTAL COWBOY

This is respectfully dedicated to the "American Cowboy." His was the saga sparked by the turmoil that followed the Civil War, and the passing of more than a century has by no means diminished the flame.

True, the old days and the old ways are but treasured memories, and the old trails have grown dim with the ravages of time, but the spirit of the cowboy lives on.

In my travels—to Texas, Oklahoma, Kansas, Nebraska, Colorado, Wyoming, New Mexico, and Arizona—I always find something that reminds me of the Old West. While I am walking these plains and mountains for the first time, there is this feeling that a part of me is eternal, that I have known these old trails before. I believe it is the undying spirit of the frontier calling, allowing me, through the mind's eye, to step back into time. What is the appeal of the Old West of the American frontier?

It has been epitomized by some as the dark and bloody period in American history. Its heroes—Crockett, Bowie, Hickok, Earp—have been reviled and criticized. Yet the Old West lives on, larger than life.

It has become a symbol of freedom, when there was always another mountain to climb and another river to cross; when a dispute between two men was settled not with expensive lawyers, but with fists, knives, or guns. Barbaric? Maybe. But some things never change. When the cowboy rode into the pages of American history, he left behind a legacy that lives within the hearts of us all.

—*Ralph Compton*

Chapter 1

Tom

There it was again, that black pit in his gut, roiling with a nameless fear. It happened every morning when Jimmy shook him awake, bringing him out of the dark dreams, in which he was always riding in an unknown land, chasing after senseless cows in every shape and color imaginable, and being chased by nameless men with mangled, twisted features that defied identification. Men with guns and knives riding dragon horses with scales and talons, calling out his name, hunting him down to take away his life, to take away his soul.

"Come on, Dag," Jimmy said in his slow, deep drawl. "Horses are under saddle and the coffeepot's burpin' like a fartin' colt."

"I'm awake, Jimmy. It's my bones that are still gettin' shut-eye."

"You ain't gonna like sunrise, Dag. The sky, I swear, is bloodred."

Felix Dagstaff had been plagued by bad weather all spring. It had been the wettest he had seen since coming to Texas fifteen years before. It was hard enough getting a herd together in rugged country, without battling water, mud, lightning, and the flurries of flash floods that roared through Palo Duro Canyon.

Dag cursed softly as he sat up, then shoved the blanket into a puddle of wool at his feet. When he stood up, both of his knees cracked, and a needling pain shot through cartilage and bone. The knees would be all right after he walked a few steps, but they stiffened up on him every time he sat or lay down for a spell.

He felt the chill right away. A fresh breeze was blowing out of the northwest, and when he turned to the east, he saw the crimson sky Jimmy Gough had warned him about. The horizon over toward Quitaque glowed like the coals in a banked furnace. It was cloudless yonder and Vulcan's flames spread as far as the eye could see from horizon to horizon, north to south.

"Damned red sky in morning," Dag muttered as he walked toward the smell of coffee and the blazing fire Jimmy had made with green mesquite and whatever dry wood he had been able to find the night before.

Gough stood silhouetted against the fire, tall and lean as a buggy whip, his battered hat the only indication that he was human and not a torn-down split-rail fence. Jimmy had a steaming tin cup in his hand, and the vapors floated up to his face like steam rising from a creek on a brisk morning.

"Here's your cup," Gough said, stretching out a long, lanky arm.

Dag took the tin cup and poured coffee into it, almost to the brim. He liked his coffee hot and strong. They always used Arbuckle's, which had a cinnamon stick in it. He didn't know if he could taste the faint cinnamon flavor, but he imagined he could, and that was good enough.

"I saw mares' tails in the sky yesterday evenin'," Gough said.

"Yeah, I saw 'em too. Won't rain today, though."

"No, not today. Might be a gully washer tonight, though."

"You can damned nigh bet on it, Jimmy." The coffee burned Dag's mouth and warmed his throat and stomach. The fire helped lessen the hurt in his knee joints. He flexed his legs, pumping each up and down in place. The joints no longer creaked, anyway. One knee felt like it was going to give out before the day was done, however. "Coffee's right bad, Jimmy. What'd you make it with, horse apples? Tastes like it's got some tar mixed in it."

"You like it strong, Dag. You can float a ten-penny nail in this batch."

"Any sign of Little Jake?" The minute he asked, Dag knew he was whistling in the wind. If Little Jake had ridden in last night, he'd be out there with him and Jimmy, cracking his lame old jokes.

"Nary," Gough said. "Maybe he went on home."

Dag blew on his coffee, drank a sip. It was still boiling hot.

"No, not Little Jake. He don't even go home to get a whuppin' no more. He cut them apron strings last year."

"Yeah, the ornery rascal," Jimmy said. "He done made our bunkhouse his kip. The boys keep runnin' him off, but he turns up every evenin', just the same."

Little Jake was a homeless boy who wandered from ranch to ranch, looking for work, looking for his mother. He was bewildered most of the time and some of the hands thought he was addled. But he was a hard worker and good with cattle. He was better with cattle than he was with people, Dag thought, even though he was fond of the boy. He felt sorry for the boy, too.

Big Jake had gone off to war and gotten himself killed. Little Jake's ma had taken up with Big Jake's brother and then they up and left one day, the both of them, without saying a word to Little Jake. They just left him, saying they were going to San Antonio and would be back in a month. Neither of them ever returned, and Jake had been waiting for them for two or three years. His family name was Bogel. His ma's maiden name was Sandora Lovitt. Jake's uncle, Dan Bogel, was a worthless piece of shit if ever there was one, Dagstaff thought.

"Well, we got to get back down into that gully this mornin'," Dag said. "I know I heard calves bawlin' down in there."

"I didn't hear nothin'," Jimmy said. "The damned wind howlin' down the Palo Duro, maybe."

"Maybe you heard your own asshole singin', Jimmy. You 'bout gassed me to death down in that gully."

"Them beans we had yesterday mornin' must have been refried more'n once or twice."

Dag kept at his coffee, lest it should get cold on him. He felt the liquid warm him from the center of his stomach outward, seeping into his extremities. He turned away from the fire because his pants were getting hot; he looked again at the dawning sky, that deep scarlet rash on the eastern horizon. The last whippoor-will broke off its leathery song with a snap as if a steel door had slammed shut and the silence rose up with all the dawn scents as the fragrances of the prairie were released by some mystical force before the dew evaporated from the wildflowers and the prickly pear cactus.

Even Jimmy seemed to revere the silence that sprang up between the two men, and Dag could hear him draw in a breath through his nostrils as if to inhale all the aromas of morning. Somewhere, far off, a cockerel crowed and the moment passed. The carnivorous maw of the sky bled out, turning to a paler crimson, and where the stars had been moments before, a yellow sky built momentum like some encroaching desert reflection in a celestial mirage.

"You still set on doin' this, Dag?"

"I am."

"It's not goin' to work. None of it."

"Look, Jimmy, we been all over this coon. I rode it last year. I got a buyer. I know the way I'm goin', and I got others throwin' in with me."

"You didn't ride it with four thousand beeves, Dag—all of 'em hungry and thirsty and a whole hell of a lot more."

Dag wasn't tired of dreaming of the trail drive. He was tired of talking about it, though. He had made up his mind. He knew it would work.

"What more, Jimmy?"

"You goin' up the Palo Duro still?"

"All the way to Amarilly, Jimmy. Purt nigh."

"Comanches still own the Palo Duro. A lot of it. The Rangers ain't drive 'em out and no one else neither."

"We'll handle that if it comes up."

"You're leavin' way too early," Jimmy said.

"We may be gone a year or two. I don't know."

"That's just it. You don't know. This time of year, them rivers are goin' to be swolled up like a plantation mammy's black belly. You're goin' to drown beeves and drovers and wind up with nothin' but an empty skull with long horns."

Dag sucked in a breath. Jimmy always sang the same old tune. He was a horse wrangler and didn't know much about cattle. And he hadn't ridden up to Cheyenne with Dag last year.

"Abilene would be better. Closer. Or even Sedalia up in Missoura. You'd get top dollar either place."

"The buyer in Cheyenne's offerin' me more."

"He won't buy cattle what ain't there, Dag."

Dag sipped more of his coffee. He was beginning to itch inside. Impatience. That was something he always had to fight against. He had been over the whole drive in his mind so many times, it often seemed as if he had already driven a large herd up to Cheyenne and come back flush with cash.

"Let's finish the coffee up and get after it, Jimmy. We should finish the count by noon and then I can call in the other hands for the gather."

"That's another thing, Dag. You can't count on nobody. Nobody round here, leastways."

"I got commitments from a bunch of good hands."

"I'm not talkin' bout them so much as Deuce. That hombre's got greed writ all over him. And he don't trust nobody 'cept hisself."

"Deuce will fill out the herd with his own cattle. We'll meet the requirements of the Cheyenne buyer."

"He wants thirty-eight hunnert head, right?"

"Right."

"Well, right now, you'll scrape the brush from here to the Rio Grande to come up with thirteen hunnert head."

"Deuce says he wants to run up twenty-five hundred. I plan on rounding up another four or five hundred head. We'll drive over four thousand head up, and wind up, maybe, with the number the buyer wants."

"Ha!" Jimmy snorted. "You could lose that extry five hunnert in one little old stampede. Not to mention them what drowns or gets snakebit, breaks their legs in prairie dog holes and such."

"I'm mighty grateful for your optimism, Jimmy. It really warms the cockles of my heart."

"Your heart ain't got no cockles, Dag. And your head ain't got no sense, neither. You watch. Deuce is a-goin' to put the boots to you, one way or another."

Dag had thought about that too. Adolph Deutsch was a hardheaded German who had built up a pretty fair herd of nearly ten thousand head of cattle. But he was a suspicious man and difficult to deal with. The cowhands had trouble with his last name and called him "Deuce," but there was another reason of the appellation—one that said something about Deutsch's character, perhaps. Adolph ran a mercantile store, a kind of trading post. He carried supplies for a lot of the outlying ranchers, but his prices were on the high side. People who bought from him said if something was marked a dollar, he would say the price had gone up and double it. "He deuces everything," the ranchers and cowhands said, and they weren't far off, Dag admitted.

The sun was edging up over the eastern horizon when Dag finished his coffee. He set his cup down. Jimmy took a final swallow and tossed the rest of his on the ground, next to the fire ring.

"We'll come back and maybe cook some breakfast," Dag said, starting toward his saddled horse.

Then the silence was shattered by a high-pitched scream that curdled the air and lifted the hackles on the backs of both men's necks.

That was when both Jimmy and Dag stopped dead in their tracks.

"Egod, Dag, that sounded like Little Jake."

"Shit," Dag said, and then he was running toward his horse.

Chapter 2

The scream came from somewhere to the west of their camp. Dag was in the saddle first, and he dug smooth-roweled spurs into the flanks of his sorrel gelding, heading for one of the gullies that marked the land and left humps of earth in low mounds as if some giant burrowing animal had dug below them. The scream lingered in his brain like a tattered ribbon of sound, chilling, gut-wrenching.

Dag knew Jimmy was right behind him. He could hear the pounding hooves of the other man's little buckskin pony, the crack of dry branches breaking, the thud of iron shoes on hard pan. The sun had cleared the horizon; horse and rider cast a long, eerie shadow in front of Dag, a dark horseman riding through a dream, through golden sand, racing, racing, but never catching up.

He saw something waving, something bright and white, white as bone, caught in the glare of the sun just above the ground. But as he rode up, Dag saw that someone was in one of the gullies waving a shirt to attract attention. He drew his six-gun, a converted Remington New Army .44 that took cartridges instead of percussion caps, and rode into the gully.

Little Jake was standing near something dark and ugly on the ground. His face was drained of blood and Dag could see that the kid was scared. His shirt—the one he had waved above his head like a flag of surrender—was off.

"Dag, it's Little Jake," Jimmy hollered behind him.

Dag reined his gelding to a halt and slid from the saddle as the horse braked. "Little Jake, what have you got yourself into?" he asked as he ran up and grabbed one of the youth's arms, the one waving the shirt.

"God amighty, Dag, just look at him. I tried to bandage him up, but the blood just kept . . . kept . . ."

The young man broke down in tears, crumpling to Dag's feet.

Dag looked at the shirt, saw that it was spattered with blood. The blood was still wet.

"You just take it easy, Little Jake."

Jimmy ran up then and hunkered down to see what was wrong with Little Jake.

Dag stepped over to the dark shape and saw that it was a man's body slumped over a rock, an arrow sticking from his back and another through his neck like a skewer.

"Jesus," Dag muttered and knelt down beside the body. Something about it looked familiar. The pale blue chambray shirt, the faded duck trousers, the worn boots, heels rounded, the battered spurs with one rowel missing on the left one.

Jimmy got up, leaving Little Jake to sit there, holding his head in his hands, all slumped over, and shivering like a dog passing peach seeds.

"Do you know who it is, Dag?"

"Yeah. Luke Pettibone from the Box M, Barry Matlee's spread. Christ."

"Egod, Luke. Ah, boy. Barry won't like it none. Luke had him a wife and kid."

Jimmy was right, Dag thought. Matlee

would have to provide for the widow and her little girl. It wasn't the law, just the custom.

"Jimmy, you pull that Sharps out and keep an eye out for me," Dag said, " 'case they's any redskins still lurkin' about. I'm going to see if I can pry anything out of Little Jake."

Jimmy mounted up and pulled his rifle from its scabbard, a Sharps carbine he'd gotten from Dag when Dagstaff returned from the war and that last battle at Palmito Hill on the Rio Grande. He rode a wide circle around the gully where they had found Little Jake and Luke, looking in all directions as mist rose from the earth like smoke lingering on a battlefield.

Dag pulled Little Jake to his feet, shook him gently to snap him out of fear and self-pity. Little Jake was sobbing, whimpering, cowering.

"Be a man, Little Jake. You got the pants scared off you, but you're whole while Luke lies there dead. I want to know what happened here."

"I-I c-can't."

"You can, son, and you will. Now damn it, pull yourself together and give me an account of all this."

When Little Jake kept blubbering, Dag drew back his right hand, swept it back over his shoulder. Little Jake's eyes widened, and he cowered, waiting for the blow, dropping his head down like some defeated prisoner standing on the gallows.

Dag slapped Little Jake with the back of his hand. Little Jake's head snapped to one side as the blow took effect.

"I'll beat it out of you, if I have to, Little Jake. Now straighten up, son, and tell me what the hell happened with you and Luke. Damn it, I haven't got time to fool around with you."

There were white streaks on Little Jake's face where Dag's fingers had landed, left an impression. The young man raised his head and looked at Dag with watery eyes, sucked in quick breaths to overcome the sobbing. Dag shook him again and Little Jake straightened his back and drew in another deep breath and held it for a moment.

"Me 'n' Luke was out early, after a cow and calf," Little Jake said in a string of halty words that poured from his mouth, "and we saw this cow a-runnin', like somethin' was a-chasin' it. Luke thought it was a coyote or maybe a bobcat. We took after it to see if we could spy a brand on its hide, and that's when we saw a bunch of red Injuns with some cattle and one of 'em chasin' after that cow. We turned tail,

but the Injun follered us, and when we got
here, I mean, we come here to hide from him
and that Injun just rode up with a bow and
slung an arrer straight at Luke. Then, before I
could figure any of it out, the Injun shot another arrer and hit Luke right in the neck. I
screamed bloody murder and the Injun lit out.
I must've scared him or somethin'."

"You made noise," Dag said. "How many Indians were in that bunch you and Luke saw?"

"A dozen at least, maybe more."

"You're lucky they didn't all jump you,
damn Comanches."

"They was Comanches all right. And fear-
some as all get out."

Dag turned away, looked upward, toward
the rim of the gully.

"Jimmy, you see anything up yonder? Little
Jake's and Luke's horses?"

There was a pause before Jimmy answered.
"I see something out there. Light's still weak.
Looks like horses, maybe."

"I'll send Little Jake up there."

Dag turned to the young man. "Little Jake,
get on my horse and ride up to where Jimmy
is. Catch up yours and Luke's horses and I'll
stay here and get these arrows out of him."

Little Jake was happy to go from that place. He climbed into the saddle on Dag's horse and rode up out of the gully.

Dag squatted down next to Luke's body. He lifted the dead man's head and placed a rock under it to hold it up. He grabbed the front end of the arrow at the neck and clamped it with his thumb and index finger. He picked up another rock and set it against the nock, squaring it and holding it firm. He pushed from the nock end as hard as he could. The arrow slid through the wound until the feathers were buried in Luke's neck. Dag set down the rock and scooted around, then pulled on the blood-wet shaft until it came free, sending Dag back on his haunches. The arrow was marked with symbols beneath the smears and streaks of blood.

Dag threw the arrow down and got up. He turned Luke's body over until it lay flat on the ground, backside down. Then he lifted him by the boots and dragged him out of the gully onto level ground. He was puffing from the exertion by then, and stood hunched over as he regained his normal breathing rhythm.

He looked around and saw Jimmy and Little Jake riding toward him, leading the two horses that had wandered off during the fracas with the

Comanche. Comanches down this far along the Palo Duro meant trouble. It also meant they were hungry. They must have seen the chuck wagons and the cowhands riding around and figured out that it was getting close to roundup time. Even a dozen Comanches could mess up the spring roundup, the bastards. Dag cursed them roundly in his mind while he waited for the two riders.

The three men lifted Luke's stiffening corpse and draped him over the saddle of his horse, with some difficulty. The horse, a bay mare, rolled its eyes and sidestepped every time they hoisted the body up to the saddle. It sidled stiff-legged in a half circle trying to avoid taking on the cargo. Its ears stiffened to twin cones, and Dag could have sworn its mane bristled just like the hair on the back of an alarmed cat. Finally, they got Luke's belly into the cradle of the saddle and both Dag and Jimmy bent him over it like a soft horseshoe, then took Luke's rope, which was tied with leather thongs to one of the D rings on the saddle, and tied his feet and hands together underneath the belly of the skittery mare.

"Little Jake," Dag said, "you take the reins and pull this horse. Hold on tight. Jimmy will ride drag and I'll lead us over to the chuck wagon where y'all spent the night. Is Matlee over yonder with y'all?"

"Yes, sir, he come in last night."

"Save you a long ride to the Box M. Barry can take care of his own. He got other hands there?"

"Yes, sir, there's—"

"I don't need a list, Little Jake. You still camped over to Rattlesnake Creek?"

"Yes, sir."

"Let's switch horses, son. You might get used to riding Nero."

Little Jake climbed down from Dag's horse and took up the reins of his own. The two men mounted their horses and Dag led out, with Little Jake on his own horse, Luke on his, and Jimmy following atop the buckskin pony.

"Wait a minute," Dag said. "I better bring those arrows."

"What for?" Jimmy asked.

"Proof, I reckon."

There were men milling around the chuck wagon, horses snorting steam and pawing the ground, whickering at the approaching riders and whinnying like a clutch of old women at a Sunday school picnic. Some of the men held coffee cups and a couple were smoking cigarettes and stamping their boots to get their circulation

up and the cold out of their toes. Two of the
men were pissing into the creek and making a
faint yellow steam rise from the cold waters.

Those standing around the fire went silent as
Dag rode up. They shifted their gaze to Luke,
astraddle his horse. Disbelief shimmered in the
quivering muscles on their faces. Barry Matlee
stepped forward. Behind him loomed the
bulky figure of Deuce Deutsch, his forbidding
scowl visible even in shadow.

"Dag, what you got there? Is that Luke?"

Dag handed him the arrow shafts.

"Son of a bitch," Matlee said.

The sun inched above the horizon, sent
golden streamers across the land and flared on
the dark statues of men who bore the deep
silence that comes in the presence of death.
One of the Matlee men choked up and let out
a soft unmanly sob.

Matlee looked up at Little Jake, his eyes blazing with a sudden anger.

"I ought to kill you, you little bastard,"
Matlee said, his right hand streaking for the
pistol on his hip.

In that one terrible moment, time seemed to
stand still as the sun raged ever higher, setting
the high, thin clouds afire in its rising.

Chapter 3

Dag leaned over from the saddle and grabbed Matlee's forearm. He dug his fingers into the soft flesh of the muscle and pushed downward so that the rancher couldn't draw his pistol.

"There's plenty of death to go around as it is, Barry. You back off. Little Jake didn't have nothing to do with what happened to Luke."

"I told them two not to go out alone this morning," Matlee said, relaxing his hand's grip on the butt of his pistol. "Damned if I didn't warn them both."

"Ain't no matter now," Dag said, his voice as soft as the disappearing dawn. "Could have been me or you, Barry. Me 'n' Jimmy was up and out awful early. Ten minutes sooner, we might have wound up like Luke there. Settle down, son."

Matlee looked up at Dag and nodded like a man too numb to speak. There was a sadness in his eyes. It flickered like a shadow darting in and out of sunlight.

"Which way did the Comanches head?" he asked.

"North. Jimmy and I camped way north of you. They got a good head start."

"How many head did they get?"

"I don't know," Dag answered. "I don't think Little Jake knows either. He was pretty shaken up."

"Ain't enough we got rain comin' tonight or tomorrow. Now we got Comanches stealin' stock."

"I don't figger they got more'n one or two head, the way they lit out. Probably a single head and they got it butchered by now."

"Shit fire, Dag, we're in a stretch to come up with enough head to drive to Cheyenne and you picked a trail what ain't no good no ways."

Dag stepped out of the saddle.

"Are you backing out, Barry?" Dag asked.

Matlee hesitated. Deuce stepped forward

and waddled his considerable weight over to where Dag and Matlee were standing.

"I'm pulling my herd out, Dagstaff," Deuce said. "This is the kind of thing I worried about ever since you told me about this drive."

"Deutsch, you're making a big mistake. You have more at stake than the rest of us. Pulling your cattle out will leave me way short."

"We're just getting started with the roundup, and already a man dead we have, and cattle stolen right from under our eyes."

"A few hungry Comanches, Deutsch, that's all. We'll probably never see them again. Besides, we'll have enough men and cattle on the drive, we can hold off a Comanche raid."

The other men, from the various ranches, including his own, gathered around, listening to every word. Dag didn't look at them, but he knew they were probably just as skeptical as Deutsch, and he granted that they had good reason. The roundup was starting off badly. His idea had been to separate the cows with fresh calves and just take the hardiest cattle up the Palo Duro and then drift them to the Goodnight-Loving Trail. Deutsch had been the hardest to convince that the drive would be both successful and profitable.

Jimmy dismounted, as well, but Little Jake remained on his horse, looking down at the assemblage in abject wonder.

"You won't drive a single head of Rocking D cattle on your wild-goose chase," Deutsch said. "I will not risk it."

Matlee cursed under his breath. "Dag, we ain't got enough head between us to go all the way to Cheyenne and come up empty."

"That's true," Dag said. "Deutsch, you promised. You accepted my offer. Are you backing out now?"

"I am. I said I would let you drive my cattle to market if you had sufficient head and there was no danger of loss."

"There's always a danger of loss in anything," Dag said, realizing his argument was weak. But without Deutsch's cattle, none of them would earn a cent. The contract called for thirty-eight hundred head of prime beef stock and he could not make the drive with less than four thousand head, factoring in losses along the way.

"I will not take that risk," Deutsch said. "My cattle the drive will not make."

When he was angry, Deutsch always put his

English in German grammatical form. And he was angry. His face was puffed up and red as a sugar beet. The cords in his neck wriggled like writhing snakes and the veins stood out like blue earthworms.

"You're awful quick to call this," Dag said. "You're hurtin' almost as bad as the rest of us, and we can't rub two nickels together. What you got up your sleeve, Deuce, besides an arm?"

"To Sedalia, in Missouri, we will drive my cattle, Felix."

"The Shawnee Trail?"

"We call it the Sedalia Trail, but the same it is, yes."

"You won't get the price I can get for you," Dag said.

"No. The thirty-five dollars a head we will get and that is enough for my herd. It is the safe way, sure."

Dag looked down at the ground and began working the toe of his boot into the dirt, scraping a smooth spot as if clearing his own mind in that same way. He tilted his foot and scraped with the edge of his boot. Then he looked up, stared into Deuce's eyes.

"Sounds to me like you already made up your mind before you came to roundup, Deuce."

"I make my mind up now."

Dag searched the faces of the men standing around them. He looked at one man, stared at him hard. The man was Sam Coker, Deuce's segundo. Coker bunched his lower lip up against his upper, then shifted his gaze to another part of the landscape.

"That right, Coker?" Dag asked. "You didn't know anything about this change of plan?"

"I go with what Mr. Deutsch says." Coker still avoided Dag's gaze.

"You were going to use us all to help you with roundup, Coker, and all the time you and Deuce had no intention of honoring our agreement."

Coker sucked in a breath.

No one spoke a word.

Dag looked back at Deutsch, an expression of contempt on his face. His eyes narrowed to dark slits.

"All right, Deuce, you called it. That's my chuck wagon there. You and your hands clear on out of here. You'll get no help from me with your damned roundup."

"But we have always done roundup together," Deutsch protested. "Who is to regulate?"

"I'll regulate our cows. You regulate your own. Now clear out."

Coker stepped forward, a scowl on his face. "Dagstaff, you're violating the law of the range here."

"You've got a nerve, Coker. Deutsch backed down on his word. Out here a man's word is the law."

"You're not leavin' us out, Dagstaff," Coker said. "We got as much right to check cattle as you do."

"Yeah? Well, not anymore, Coker. Pack it up."

Coker's rage surged up so quickly nobody there was prepared for it. He balled up his fists and rushed toward Dagstaff. He drove a fist into Dag's face, knocking him backward. Blood spurted from Dag's nose and he reeled under the impact. Then all hands erupted and joined in the fray. Coker drove in for another blow, but Dag shook off the pain and slammed Coker with a roundhouse right that caught him in the left jaw, staggering him.

Deutsch went after Dag, a fist cocked to

hammer a blow to his face. Dag moved his head and Deutsch's fist grazed his chin, knocking his head back slightly. Dag drove a fist into Deutsch's paunch, saw the man quiver and absorb the blow as he expelled air from his lungs.

Fists flew from every direction after that. Men yelled and pummeled one another with flailing arms. There was biting, clawing, and kicks to the groin as the fight turned into a wild melee. Matlee squared off with Coker and the two exchanged punches. Blood squirted from noses and ears. Dag grappled with the heavier Deutsch, who was trying to wrestle him to the ground. Breathing heavily, Dag drove a fist into Deutsch's groin. The man grunted in pain and doubled over. Dag hit him with a powerful uppercut, but the two went down, rolling away from the center of the fight, both men lashing at each other with their fists and open hands.

Jimmy Gough smashed Coker with a straight right to the throat. Coker gasped for air, and a wheezing sound issued from his throat, while his lips started to turn blue. Jimmy felt someone climb on his back and turned, trying to shake the man off. He felt arms wrap around his neck. He drove an elbow into his attacker's gut and heard a groan. He shook himself free and stepped away, drawing his pistol.

Jimmy fired into the air.

"That's enough," he yelled. "I'll shoot the next man that throws a punch."

The men stopped fighting and looked at Gough, whose eyes blazed like red-hot coals.

Jimmy swung the snout of his pistol toward Coker. "You'll be the first to die, Coker," Gough said. "Now you heard Dag. Clear out, or you'll join Luke draped over your own saddle."

"Don't shoot, Jimmy," Coker said. "We'll go, but you watch your back, hear?"

"So you're a back shooter, eh, Coker? Well, if you want to call it, call it now. I'm ready to open the ball, you son of a bitch."

The ensuing silence told Dag that the fight was over—unless somebody made a terrible mistake and called Jimmy out. He could see that Gough was ready to shoot the first man who made an aggressive move. He dusted himself off, slapping his trousers and shirt.

"All right, Jimmy," Dag said, "you made your point. Let's drop it. No more threats, Coker. Just pack up and ride off. Deuce, you get your men out of here. Barry, get one of your men to take Luke back home. We've had enough grief for one day."

Deuce nodded, swiping a sleeve across bloody lips. "You pay for this, Dagstaff," he said, huffing for breath. "By God, you pay dear for the trouble you bring."

Dag drew his pistol. He aimed the barrel at Deutsch and cocked it. In the silence, men sucked in their breath and froze in their tracks. Off in the distance a meadowlark trilled.

"We go," Deutsch said, and turned to Coker. "We go back, Coker. Tomorrow the roundup we will make."

Dag watched as Coker and his men gathered their cups and mounted up in sullen silence. Matlee took the reins of Luke's horse from Little Jake, who had sat his horse watching the whole thing, dumbfounded at the sudden eruption of violence.

Deutsch and the men of the Rocking D rode off to the east, into the glare of the sun.

Dag let the hammer down on his pistol and holstered it. Jimmy slid his own pistol back into its holster and let out a long breath.

No one spoke for a long time, as if they all were wondering what to do next, as if wondering who had been right, who had won, who had lost.

Chapter 4

Some of the longhorns that spring were as wild as the beasts of far-off Africa. Chad Myers and Carl Costello, two of Dag's hands riding for his D Slash spread, were driving eight of them out of a brushy draw under a hot sun that boiled all of the salt out of them and burned their already leathered faces to the crispness of fried bacon. Chad's little cow pony, Ruff, was working back and forth like a dog with a bone, while Carl's horse, Lulu, crowded the rear, sawing back and forth to keep the cattle in line.

The cattle streamed onto level land, moving their heads back and forth to look over their surroundings. Their legs were caked with mud, which had accumulated on the ground from the recent rains. Chad edged toward the leader to let the cow know that if it bolted, he would run it down. He slipped the lariat from its thongs and shook out a loop, just in case. Carl put his horse into a sideways sidle and bunched the cows up from the rear. The cattle halted in a bunch and Chad let them think it over.

"This ought to be the last of it," he told Carl.

"Yup. We're always the last in."

"These ain't seen a horse all winter, let alone a rider."

"Maybe a lot longer than that. Check them brands."

Carl noted that four of the cows had the D Slash brand, which was Dag's. Two were Box M cattle, belonging to Matlee. One was a Rocking D, Deutsch's brand. The seventh had no brand at all.

"Cut out the Rocking D and let's head 'em in for the tally," Chad said.

Carl moved the cattle and guided his horse to cut out the Deutsch cow. An hour later, they arrived at the main herd, which stretched from horizon to horizon. They waved to Dag and Jimmy, Ed Langley and Doofus Wallace, who were tending the smaller bunch of cattle separated from the main herd. Dag was tallying the cattle, with Jimmy looking on as a backup checker. Wallace and Langley were letting the counted cows join the main herd, holding back the rest.

"Just run 'em in behind," Dag called to Chad.

The two men let their cows join the smaller herd, then rode flank on the rest until the tallying was done. The ground was still wet from the heavy rains, so there was little dust that day. Some of the mud was starting to cake up under the baking heat of the sun. They rode up to Dag and Jimmy.

"That's the last of them, boss. All we could find." Chad took off his hat and wiped his forehead with his bandanna.

"It don't look good," Dag said. "About half Matlee's and half ours."

"What's the tally?" Carl asked.

"A shade under twelve hundred head."

"Shit." Chad put his hat back on, squared it, and crumpled the crown with a pinch of deft fingers.

"Let's go over to the chuck wagon and talk about this," Dag said.

The whole herd moved slowly, and as Dag

rode the length of it, he talked to the other herders and told them to leave the cows to graze and join them at the chuck wagon next to Rattlesnake Creek. The herd began to swell and expand as the riders left, the cattle grazing on new shoots of green grass. It was like watching a river widen and extend its banks, Dag thought. And the herd was pointed north.

"One of them cows warn't branded," Chad told Dag as he rode alongside. "We cut out a Rocking D."

"Good. Too bad we can't use a running iron on those."

Chad laughed. "I could make one real quick."

"We'll do this by the book, Chad," Dag said.

"I'll bet we ran into a thousand head of Deuce stock on this last go-round."

"I counted a few hundred myself. Deuce will come out all right at thirty-five dollars a head in Sedalia."

"He might get forty."

"We'll get fifty."

The men from two ranches, the Box M and the D Slash, gathered at the chuck wagon. They all dismounted and ground-tied their horses. They knew they were not through riding for the day. There was an air of anticipation among them as they whispered their concerns to one another and looked at Dag for a sign of what he might be going to say.

"Gather round," Dag said to the men.

The hands and Matlee formed a semicircle around Dag. In the chuck wagon, Bill Finnerty, the cook they called "Fingers" and his daughter, Jo, sat on the buckboard seat overlooking the cluster of men.

"Well," Dag said, "that's the gather yonder. Headed north. We'll start the drive in two days."

"How many head you got, Dag?" Matlee called out.

"I'll get to that, Barry. Just hold your horses."

Laughter rippled through the assemblage like a nervous current.

"We'll have shifts watch the herd, giving you all a chance to go home, say goodbye, and pack for the trip. Bring rifles, pistols, ammunition, canteens, bedrolls, extra tack, your favorite grub. Extra horses. I want the remuda to have some sixty to sixty-five head. Fingers won't spoil you on this trip. And neither will Josephine."

More laughter, less nervous this time.

Then one of Matlee's men, Fred Reilly, spoke up. "You're not takin' no woman on this drive, are you, Dagstaff?"

"Where Fingers goes, his daughter goes. Yes, Jo is coming with us, and you should all be mighty grateful. And maybe you'll learn some manners along the way, Reilly."

There was a trickle of laughter, but it was plain to see that a lot of the men objected to having a woman along on a trail drive, especially one that would last as long as this one. There were some muttering and grumbling, but it died down quickly.

"Make your own choices for the rotation. Half here, half going home. Then the same tomorrow. I know, I know, some of you won't have as much time to kiss the missus as the others, but you can quarrel about that when you divide up."

A chuckle or two broke out, but the seriousness of the moment was not lost on anyone there.

"Expect to be gone most of a year," Dag said, and waited for the effect of his words on all the men.

"I don't think we have near enough cattle to make the drive," Matlee said, a moment later. "Not enough to pay for a drive even to Abilene or Sedalia."

"Barry," Dag said, "you really got that head count stuck in your craw, don't you?"

Dag said it amiably and the crowd laughed, but then it turned serious. Some more grumbling began to break out. Dag held up his hands to quiet the men down.

"It's a damned good question, Dag," Jimmy said. "A lot of us have been wonderin' what you mean to do with this scrawny little herd."

The men grunted in agreement with Gough.

"This from a man who doesn't know one end of a cow from the other," Dag said. "He's a mighty fine horse wrangler, but I caught him trying to milk a steer the other day."

More laughter erupted, and Dag felt some of the tension subside this time.

"All right, you deserve an answer, Barry, and here's what I've worked out. Before you all go protesting, hear me out."

"We're waiting, Dag," Matlee said. "You've got the deal."

"And all the cards," Dag quipped. Then, in

a more serious tone, he began speaking. He spoke very slowly and loud enough for every man to hear.

"When I made the trip to Cheyenne last year, I saw a lot of stray cattle. I saw a lot of unbranded cattle. Now what we're going to do is forage all the way through Texas. Box M men can brand the cattle they bring in, and my men will burn the D Slash into those they bring to the herd. I'll pay seventy-five cents extra for each head brought in. Now there are millions of cattle in Texas and not all of them wear brands. I expect this herd to swell to the number we need by the time we hit the Red River."

"Impossible," someone said.

"It's going to be work—I grant you that," Dag said. "But by God, we can do it and we're going to do it."

"You really think we can find nearly three thousand head of cattle on the drive?" Matlee asked.

"I do. And I'm going to show all of you how to do it, starting on the first day of the drive, two days from now."

There were expressions of disbelief among a number of the men. Dag stood his ground and let the dissension die down.

"Now one other thing," Dag said, "there's going to be only one trail boss on this drive. He will have the final say on anything that comes up. He's the best there is, and I want you to know that even I will follow his orders. I've given this a lot of thought and I've talked to the man and he's agreed to come with us and lead us to Cheyenne."

"You're not going to be trail boss?" Jimmy Gough asked.

"No, I'll be out with all of you, rounding up more head to fill our contract."

"Well, who the hell is this trail boss?" Reilly asked. "We might not like the son of a bitch."

More laughter.

Again, Dag waited until there was absolute silence.

Then he dropped the bomb, knowing there would be an explosion. "Jubal Flagg," he said.

The air turned blue with curses, and for a few moments, Dag thought he might have a riot on his hands. But all he did was stand there and smile with a confidence he knew he didn't have. Jubal Flagg was probably the most hated man in that part of the country. But he was also the best.

Chapter 5

Dag stood on the back porch of his adobe house staring past the outhouse and garden to beyond the empty pastures at the flaming sunset. The magnificent glow stretched from horizon to horizon like the banked fires of a gigantic furnace. Tomorrow would be a good day, he thought, and hoped the next one would be too. He thought of the others who worked on his ranch, knowing they were home, as well. The Box M hands and his own had decided to take separate shifts. Tomorrow, he and his men would relieve Matlee's so they could pack and say goodbye to their families and friends.

The final tally that day had wound up being

1,376 head of cattle, more than he had figured. He was still a long way from having enough for the long drive to Cheyenne, but in his heart, he knew he would swell the herd to nearly four thousand head.

It was a big gamble, he knew, but with Flagg running the outfit, they had a better than even chance of picking up enough unbranded cattle to fulfill the contract.

"Felix, supper's ready."

Dag turned and saw his wife standing in the open doorway, a smile on her tired face. The woman worked hard, but time had been kind to her. She was still beautiful, with her auburn hair and sparkling blue eyes, her sculptured face radiant with Grecian symmetry and grace. Her apron bulged out with the baby growing inside her. Alas, he would not be there to see it born, come September.

"Thanks, Laura. Would you just look at that sunset?"

She laughed. "I see it every day when you're gone," she said, "and I wonder if you're looking at it the same time as I am."

He followed her into the house, into the rich smells of her kitchen, to the table laid out for supper in the center of the room, still magically cool despite the heat of the woodstove at one end of the room. Steam drifted up through the cone of golden light shining from the overhead oil lamp. He sat down at the head of table; Laura sat by his side. They bowed their heads and Dag spoke the prayer he always said at supper.

"Heavenly Father," he intoned, "we thank you for the food at our table that you have so graciously provided. We thank you for the life you have given us, and the home wherein we dwell. Amen."

"Amen," Laura echoed, and they began to eat. She had prepared roast beef, potatoes, green beans, biscuits, and gravy. They drank strong tea, which they only had on special occasions, a gift from Laura's mother, who lived in San Antonio.

"When are you leaving, Felix?" she asked.

"Oh, didn't I tell you?"

"No, you did not. I know that look in your eyes, though. And when I saw the hands coming back tonight, I knew you had finished roundup."

"Day after tomorrow."

"Do you have enough cattle to make the drive?"

"Not yet. We'll get more on the way to Amarillo."

"A big gamble."

"Yes," he said.

"When will you be back?"

"Next spring, I reckon."

"So long? The baby's due in September."

"I know. It's a long ride. But you'll have Carmelita to help you. Jorge will be with me, so she'll be able to be with you until we get back."

Jorge Delgado was one of Dag's best cowhands. His wife, Carmelita, worked for Laura, helping her with the washing, the cooking, the housecleaning. He had sent her home so that Jorge could say goodbye.

"Is Jo going?"

And there it was, the question Dag had been dreading. Laura knew as well as he that Bill Finnerty's daughter went everywhere with him. He was a widower and Jo was a big help to him. She was always at roundup, and at the big picnics they had on the Fourth of July.

"Yes, dear, Jo is going. Of course. You know that."

"That girl will be trouble, Felix."

"What do you mean? She's no trouble that I know of."

Laura's eyes flashed and then seethed with the smoky haze that marked a smoldering fire within her.

"That gal took a fancy to you ever since she had pippins on her chest. And now that she's a woman, she's got her sights set on you, Felix. Don't tell me you haven't noticed."

"I haven't noticed, Laura. Honest."

"Well, I'm telling you, Jo's going along on this drive for one reason."

"Oh, pshaw, Laura. You make mountains out of anthills."

"That's molehills, Felix, and I'm not. Jo is how old now? Twenty?"

"Maybe."

"She's twenty-two, Felix, and you know damned well how old she is. She flirts with you at every picnic, every race, every get-together. You may not have the roving eye, but that woman wants to find out what you got in your britches. I know."

Dag flushed with embarrassment. Jo was pretty, but he was too old for her. And he was married.

"Laura, don't make something out of nothing. You're my woman and I'm your man. I don't plan on sparking that girl. Far as I'm concerned, she's just a cook, like her pa. She'll be treated as such."

Laura was still fuming when they finished supper. Dag could see that she had been talking about Jo in her mind the whole time they sat at the table in silence. The rest of the conversation could erupt at any moment and he'd catch hell for something he hadn't done and didn't intend to do.

Soon after Laura finished washing and drying the dishes, they heard dogs barking. Laura went to the front window and looked out into the darkness.

"Felix," she said, "someone's coming up our road. I can see their shapes by the moonlight."

Dag went to the window.

"Two riders," he said.

And moments later, they heard hoofbeats as the riders approached. Horses in the corrals whinnied.

"Now who could that be at this hour?" she asked, as she and Dag stood looking out the window.

"Hard to tell, but they're in an all-fired hurry."

The riders stopped at the hitch rail, dismounted, and wrapped their reins around the top pole.

"It's Deuce," he said, "and Coker."

"I'll make some coffee. I wonder what they want. Maybe Deuce changed his mind and is going to let you drive his cattle to Cheyenne."

"That man doesn't change his mind," Dag said. "Once he makes it up, it turns to hard stone."

Dag opened the door. Lamplight spilled out onto the porch, painted a soft yellow carpet.

"Deuce," Dag said, "Sam, come on in."

"Felix," Deutsch said with noncommittal curtness. Coker said nothing. The two men entered the front room and Dag closed the door behind them.

"Sit down, Adolph. Laura's putting coffee on to boil. Or would you like some elderberry?"

"No, we will not long stay," Deutsch said. But he did sit down on the divan. Coker sat next to him. Both men took off their hats, but held them in their hands. Coker ran the brim of his hat through his fingers in a circular motion. Deutsch set his hat on the arm of the divan.

Dag sat down in a chair facing the two men.

"Have you eaten?" he asked. "Laura can set out plates for you, I'm sure."

"We have eaten, Felix, but settle well the food does not."

Coker's face was drawn tight, with anger seething just below the surface of his visage, as if something were boiling in his mind and he was just holding back to keep from opening an ugly valve that would spew it all out. Dag noticed that both men wore pistols. He knew that Deuce seldom carried a weapon.

"Maybe you ate too much, Adolph."

"I think not," Deuce said.

"I don't suppose you've changed your mind about putting your herd in with ours for the drive to Cheyenne, Adolph. We're leaving day after tomorrow."

"Maybe you will not," Deutsch said. "I am closing my trading post. Supplies, we will not sell you, Felix."

"Why? Don't you want to supply us with staples, make money for yourself?"

"You know damned well why, Dagstaff," Coker said, his fury spilling over.

Laura, perhaps hearing the venom in Coker's voice, entered the room, forcing a cheery air.

"Coffee will be ready soon," she said brightly.

"We won't be staying for coffee, ma'am," Coker said, "thanking you all the same."

Deutsch nodded at Laura, half stood up, out of politeness, but sat down again right away.

"We go now pretty soon," Deutsch said.

Dag could smell the coffee and he knew the two guests could, as well. This was as close to rude as he had ever seen Deutsch around a woman, and he wondered what was eating the man.

"Deuce," Dag said, "maybe you'd better tell me straight out why you rode over here tonight. Was it just to tell me you weren't going to sell me supplies tomorrow?"

"No," Deutsch said. "I come to tell you, Mr. Dagstaff, that away with this you will not get." Dag knew that the "Mr." was thrown in because Laura was standing there. Deuce even glanced sheepishly at Laura when he said it.

"Get away with what?"

Before Deutsch could answer, Laura spoke up. "Perhaps I should leave," she said. "If you're not going to stay for coffee, Mr. Deutsch . . ."

"Yes, Laura, go on," Dag said. "Mr. Deutsch is leaving."

Laura left the room. Dag heard the coffeepot clang on the iron stove, and then it was silent as Deutsch glared at him. His bruises were still showing on his face and Coker had some new scars on his nose and cheekbones.

"What am I supposed to have gotten away with?" Dag asked.

Deutsch's face twisted into a grimace that quickly became florid with hate. His eyes bulged, and his neck swelled like that of a bull in the rut. His thick lips protruded from his face as he struggled to find the words to express his anger.

"This morning, my top hands, Manny Chavez and Don Horton, drew their pay. I can't make the drive without replacing them."

"And you blame me, Deuce? Hell, I didn't hire 'em on, and I don't think Matlee did either."

Coker stood up. "You're a damned liar, Dag."

Then Deutsch stood up too. Both men's hands hovered over the butts of their pistols like fluttering hawks.

"You can see I'm not armed," Dag said. "And I'm not lying. I don't know anything about Manny and Don drawing their pay at the Rocking D. I wouldn't mind having them on my drive. Hell, I was hoping to have your cattle along to fill out the herd—you know that."

"Felix is not armed, but I am."

All heads turned to look at Laura, who was standing just inside the front room, with a shotgun at her shoulder. As Deutsch and Coker stood there, frozen with surprise and shock, Laura thumbed back both hammers.

Click. Click.

Chapter 6

Laura had the shotgun aimed directly at Deutsch and Coker. The sound of the hammers clicking back to full cock was followed by a thick silence.

"I killed a copperhead this morning," Laura said.

Deutsch swallowed hard and Coker's mouth opened as his jaw dropped down.

"We were not going to shoot your husband, Laura," Deutsch said.

"You looked like you were, Adolph," she said.

"No, no, no," Deutsch said. "To beat him, only, I was wanting, eh? For to pay what to me he has done."

"Felix didn't do anything to you," she said.

"Laura, put the shotgun down," Dag said. "Deuce, you and Coker back off. Sit down and let's talk this out."

"I'll put it down when they sit down, Felix," Laura said, a muscle moving along her jawline, her eyes narrowed, a look of determination on her face. Deutsch blanched and sat down quickly. Coker sucked in a breath, but kept his mouth shut. He too sat back down on the divan.

Laura lowered the barrel of the shotgun and snicked the hammers back down to half-cock.

"Now," Dag said, "why in hell do you blame me for your hands quitting, Adolph? I swear I had nothing to do with it."

"Jubal Flagg you have hired, no?"

"He's going to be my trail boss, yes. But he's not due to ride in until tomorrow."

"Well, this morning, he was at my ranch. And to my men, he was talking. And then my two best hands—they did leave with him. From me this is stealing."

Dag sat back in his chair. Laura moved around the end of the divan and stood next to Dag's chair, both hands still gripping the shotgun.

"So you see," she said, "my husband didn't

have anything to do with those men leaving, Adolph. You shouldn't accuse someone without proof."

"Then you will send my men back?" Deutsch asked.

Dag sat there, staring at Deutsch, mulling over this new situation. He knew how valuable both Manny and Don were; both were exceptional cowhands. Manny was a top-notch vaquero who had grown up with the wily longhorn, and Don knew cattle so well, he could almost read their thoughts. Both men seemed to have a rare kinship with the longhorn. They treated the animals with respect, but they also commanded obedience and trust from their charges when herding, branding, doctoring, and everything else they did with cows.

"I'll tell you, Adolph, at another time maybe, or another place, I might have sent Manny and Don packing the minute Flagg brought them up to me. But you went back on your word with me. You broke a promise. Whatever's happened since then, you've brought on yourself. I can use those two men, and evidently Flagg and I think alike. Flagg is the best cowman who ever forked a horse, and if he picked those men to come with us on our drive north, I trust his judgment. You, I don't trust. In fact, I don't even like you. So you and Coker get your asses out of my house right now, or I may tell Laura to dust you off with that scattergun, after all."

"You son of a bitch," Coker said, and started to rise from the divan.

Laura lifted the shotgun, aimed it at Coker from the hip, and pulled back both hammers to full cock.

Click. Click.

"We go now," Deutsch said, his face paling beneath the bruises. "Sam, you come."

Both men got up slowly.

Dag stood up.

"First, I give you a little something, Felix. Maybe you think you won this one battle, eh? But the good cards I still hold."

As the two men passed by Laura and Dag, Deutsch reached into the inside pocket of his coat and drew out an envelope. He handed it to Dag. Then he and Coker marched out through the front door, leaving it open behind them.

Laura walked to the door; she watched the two men mount up and ride away. She closed the door and latched it tight. She lowered the hammers on the shotgun and breathed a sigh of relief.

"What did Deutsch give you?" she asked, as she came up to her husband, the shotgun pointed at the floor.

"I don't know."

Dag opened the envelope. There were papers inside, which he drew out and glanced at hurriedly. He riffled through the first three and then came to the last, which was written in a different hand and very short.

"What is it?" Laura craned her neck to look at the papers in Dag's hand.

Dag swore and handed her the sheaf of papers.

"Oh, my," she said. "That devil."

"He's got me over a barrel now," Dag said, "that damned Deutsch."

"You? Us," she said. "We'd better talk this over, Felix."

"Yeah. That makes the drive even more important now."

She leaned the shotgun against the wall and took Dag's hand. She led him to the divan, where they both sat down. She reached over and turned up the wick on the lamp.

"You know what happened, don't you?" he said.

"It looks as if Adolph bought our mortgage from Elmer McGee. This morning. Elmer's always been fine if we've been a little short on the mortgage payments, or late."

The first three pages contained a reference to Dagstaff's original contract with McGee, a description of the property, and terms of the mortgage. It also divulged that, for a certain sum, McGee transferred ownership of the mortgage over to Adolph Deutsch. To the Dagstaffs, it was a devastating document.

"I know. Did you read Adolph's note?"

"Glanced at it."

She held the last page up to the lamp, leaned over, and read it.

"Adolph says that if we miss next year's payment, or if we are short, he will foreclose on our property," she said, her tone sober, laden with a deep sadness.

"He means it too, sugar," Dag said. "Deutsch will be all over us like ugly on a bear if we're a minute late."

"Can we do it?" she asked, her voice soft, pleading.

Dag sighed as he drew in a breath and let it

out. "I don't know. It all depends on how the drive goes, how soon we get back. It depends on a lot of things."

"Why would Elmer do such a thing? He's always been the nicest man, ever since we bought this land from him."

"Elmer's a businessman. He's got holdings in Amarillo, San Antonio. He was a banker, you know. Before he went into dairy ranching, raising cotton. Lord knows, he's rich as Croesus."

"But why would he sell our mortgage to Adolph? He must have had a reason."

Dag tried to summon up all that he knew about Elmer McGee. Just before the war, he had bought up a lot of old Spanish land grants all along Palo Duro Canyon. Like Dag, he had ridden with Colonel John Salmon Ford, old Rip Ford, in the Cavalry of the West. Elmer had been wounded before the last battle at Palmito Hill and had gone back to Amarillo. While in the cavalry, he told Dag that he'd sell him land for a good price after the war and he had done just that.

"All I can think of is that Adolph has something on Elmer, and he forced the sale of that mortgage. You know Adolph is a very shrewd businessman. He's got that trading post, which he took over after the one at Quitaque went under. He sells mercantile and other goods to all the ranchers around here. Adolph's probably richer than Elmer by now."

"I still think Elmer should have told us first."

"I would have thought so, hon," Dag said, "which makes me think that Adolph has something on Elmer."

"Blackmail?"

"Maybe. You know Adolph sold cotton during the war, and Elmer raised a hell of a lot of cotton. Maybe Elmer sold to the wrong side a time or two."

"No, Elmer wouldn't do that, would he?"

Dag looked at Laura, a tenderness in his eyes. He could see that she was on the brink of tears, almost ready to break down and cry on his shoulder. She was good with the money, but she took disappointments pretty hard.

"He might," Dag said. "If he was pushed hard enough—or, if he had something else at stake, something that Deutsch knew about. A lever that Deutsch knew how to operate for his own benefit."

The two looked at each other with a sudden flash of understanding.

"Let me see those papers again," Dag said.

She didn't hand them to him, but held on to one side of the papers, while Dag turned the pages. On page three were the signatures.

And there, next to those of Elmer McGee, and Adolph Deutsch, was the notary stamp. The signature was H. McGee. And beneath the stamp and the two signatures were those affirmations of the two witnesses, Sam Coker and Helga McGee.

"That little bitch," Laura said.

"We should have known," Dag said. "Elmer married Helga, and she's very close to her father, Adolph. Elmer adores her."

"And Helga adores her father," Laura said.

"Yes, the little bitch."

They both laughed. But the laughter faded quickly.

Laura pored over the papers again. "I feel betrayed," she said.

"You can't blame Elmer, Laura. Helga is a beautiful young woman and Elmer is older than I am. He probably doesn't have that many years left. I know that wound he got in the war has worn him down. He doesn't eat right; he doesn't sleep well. Helga is the light of his life."

"His miserable life," Laura said bitterly. "Oh, people!"

"People will disappoint you, hon, more often than not."

"I'm very worried now about the drive to Cheyenne. You're short of cattle and it's so far away."

"Laura, I'm not going to give up. I'm not going to lie down and play dead because of Deutsch's treachery. I'll make the drive. I'll find the cattle we need. And I'll be back in time to pay off the mortgage."

"Pay it off?"

"Every cent of it."

"I love you, Felix," she said. They embraced and she squeezed him hard against her.

That night, they made love as if it were their last night on earth. They were like two lovers in ancient Pompeii, with the volcano Vesuvius rumbling in the background just before it erupted and buried all in the town alive.

Chapter 7

Jubal Flagg, along with Manuel Chavez and Don Horton, rode up to the herd late the next afternoon, to find Dag and his men holding the herd on a patch of grass only two miles from where the cattle had been on the previous day under Barry Matlee's supervision.

"I want this herd to start moving as soon as the sun sets," Flagg said, as he stepped down from his horse Ranger, a tall black Missouri trotter that had been gelded.

"But Matlee and his cowhands won't be back until tomorrow," Dag said.

"I don't give a damn," Flagg said. "This herd is moving tonight. Barry can catch up with us. We'll leave a wide enough trail."

"We're not out of grass here."

"No, but you want to build this herd up, Dag, and we're going to start tonight. I want you to give me two of your dumbest cowhands, right after dark. They'll come with me, Don and Manny."

"What do you aim to do, Jubal?"

"I'm going to teach them something, and then they can teach the rest of your hands. We're, by God, going to build the damnedest herd that ever left the Caprock, and drive the sons of bitches up the Palo Duro."

Flagg was an imposing figure. He stood a shade over six feet tall, with shoulders that were as wide as an ox yoke. Square-jawed, clean-shaven, he had dark brown eyes that were like twin gun barrels. His face was chiseled to a lean hardness that matched the rest of his body. His tan was deep, weathered like the soil that lined the Palo Duro Canyon, dark as old bronze. He wore a crumpled, weather-beaten felt hat and carried a Colt .44/40 on his hip. A big Sharps Yellow Boy rifle jutted from the scabbard attached to his saddle. And Dag knew he had two other pistols in his saddle bags, a Smith & Wesson .32, a belly gun, and another Colt .44, which matched the one he carried.

He wore a light blue chambray shirt, heavy duck trousers, and a red bandanna around his neck. A string to a sack of makings dripped from his shirt pocket, and he constantly chewed on a twist of strong tobacco, which he could spit, when chewed, with accuracy for a distance of at least ten feet. He took a pocket-knife from his pants pocket and cut off a chunk of twist and slid it into the side of his mouth as he looked at the cattle grazing all around them.

Three riders circled the herd at a leisurely pace, while other hands worked on their tack and began to shake out bedrolls.

Flagg spat a plume of tobacco. "They won't need those bedrolls tonight, Dag," he said. "And you tell Fingers to feed 'em light tonight and be ready to move ten miles ahead of the herd right after he's served the vittles. We'll breakfast at the Foster ranch come morning."

"You give me a lot of orders, Jubal."

"That's what you hired me for, Dag. Did you bring the cash?"

"Yep," Dag said. "Scratched up all I could. Had to have Laura empty her cookie jar."

"Give me some now, then."

"How much?"

"Fifty or sixty ought to do it for now."

"What for?"

"I'll be buying some cattle along the way, just so we stay within the law."

Dag counted out sixty dollars and handed the bills to Flagg. Jubal folded them and stuck them in the left front pocket of his trousers.

"Now hop to it, Dag. I want to see those two men I'm going to ride with tonight."

Dag thought of whom he might tell to go with Flagg. He had a pair of fairly new hands he thought would fit the bill.

Jimmy Gough was still wrestling with the growing remuda. Gough had brought in a dozen horses that morning, then had left to bring in a half dozen more. Matlee was supposed to bring more in the morning, but they still needed to find more that could make the long trip. Dag wanted at least sixty-five horses, and they all had to be sound, freshly shod, with good bottoms and none lame or otherwise afflicted. The men were close, but needed a few more, which Matlee had promised to bring the next day. Jimmy was putting on hobbles with the help of the two men Dag had in mind to go with Flagg.

"Jimmy," Dag called, "can you spare those two new wranglers helping you?"

"Them two ain't horse wranglers by any stretch of the imagination. You can have 'em both, Dag. One of 'em's classy as a pig on ice and t'other is a pure fumble-fingered fool. Neither one of 'em understands two words of English." Jimmy turned to face the two boys, who were down on their knees trying to set hobbles on the same horse. "Pancho, you and Cholo go on over yonder with Mr. Dagstaff. *Vete pronto allá.*"

The two boys muttered something in Spanish, but Dag couldn't hear it. They walked over as if they had all the time in the world. Their pants and shirts were covered with sweat, and the sweat had caked the dirt that clung to their clothing.

"Dag, are these two wetbacks cowboys?" Flagg asked.

"Sure, Jubal. They're young, but they're good with cows. They're just not too good with horses yet."

"Can they ride without being tied on with rope?"

Dag laughed. "Yeah, they can ride. Jimmy's just right particular, that's all."

"Boys, come here," Flagg said. "You speak English?"

Both young men nodded.

"What's your name, feller?" Flagg asked the taller of the two.

"Paco Noriega."

"And, you, what's your name?"

"Ricardo Mendoza."

"How come Jimmy called you Pancho and Cholo."

"He don't like us much," Paco said. "He knows our names. He makes fun of us."

"You know cows?" Flagg asked.

"Yes, the cows, we know them," Paco said.

"Fine, you boys will ride with me tonight. We're going to steal some cows. I'm going to teach you boys how to rustle cattle."

"Oh, no, we do not steal," Ricardo said. "We are honest men."

"They'll do," Flagg said to Dag. To the two Mexicans, he said, "Don't worry. We're going to rustle cattle the legal way."

"Okay, Ricardo, Paco, you saddle two horses to ride," Dag said. "Bring some rope. We'll light out right after the sun goes down."

"Yes, sir," both boys chorused. They ran off to catch their horses.

"You could have picked me a better pair than those two, Dag."

"You wanted two of the dumbest. They've had schooling and they do speak English. But they can't count and sometimes you have to tell them twice to do something that's a mite complicated."

"That's real good, Dag. I'd rather work with boys who want to learn than with men who think they know it all."

"I still don't know what you have in mind, Jubal, but I like the legal part. Just keep in mind that I can't afford to buy the cattle I need for this drive."

"That's exactly what I'm keeping in mind, Dag. Don't you worry about a thing, hear?"

Flagg left to look over the herd. Dag walked over to Jimmy, who had just finished hobbling the last horse.

"You're going to have to take those hobbles off right after sunset, Jimmy."

"Huh?"

"Flagg wants us to move the herd ten miles north tonight."

"Tonight?"

"Yeah. What do you think?"

"Well, we've got us a full moon, or near-bouts. We can do it, I reckon. Matlee will wonder where in hell we went."

"By the time he gets here tomorrow, he'll know."

"Who's taking the lead?" Jimmy asked.

"I am. Flagg's going off to round up more cattle."

Jimmy snorted.

"You don't like Jubal much, do you, Jimmy?"

"I don't know many who do."

"Why?"

Jimmy looked down at his feet, kicked a clod of dirt. "I don't know a man like Jubal Flagg," Gough said. "He's hard. Not just outside, but inside. He don't give no leeway. You know he hanged one man."

"I heard that," Dagstaff said. "A rustler, wasn't it?"

"Horse thief, yeah. When he was working at the Z Bar."

"So?"

"He horsewhipped a man for mistreating a cow when he worked at the Circle S. Near killed him."

"I don't hold with mistreating animals either, Jimmy."

"They say he shot a man over to Corpus one time. Over a woman."

"Rumors, Jimmy."

"Well, he sets hisself up as judge, jury, and executioner a mite too much to suit me, Dag."

"I asked him about that, you know."

"No, I didn't know. What did he say?"

"He said he did what he did because, at the time, he was the only law around. He said we can't have any kind of society without laws. And if there's no law around and you see a man commit a crime, you're both the law and society."

"That sounds like prime bullshit to me, Dag."

"Maybe so. But he's the best there is at driving cattle, handling men."

"He handles men because they're scared of him."

"Are you scared of him, Jimmy?"

"Hah. He don't scare me none."

"Good. Because Flagg's the boss of this outfit and I don't want any trouble about his authority."

"If Flagg speaks for you, I foller him. But if

he tells me to do something that's wrong for the horses, I'll buck him."

"You're the head wrangler, Jimmy. That won't change."

"That's good enough for me."

After supper, Dag got the herd moving. The longhorns bellowed and groaned as they set out in the darkness, with the moon just clearing the horizon. He had a good lead cow, and once the entire herd was moving, they formed a river under the rising moon, a steady flow over the pewtered land, with the outriders flanking them like ghost men on dark horses.

Flagg, along with the men he had picked for the night's work, rode off to the west and disappeared in the darkness. The chuck wagon rumbled along well behind the herd, its pots and pans clanging softly like a chorus of distant cowbells. The wagon was invented by Charlie Goodnight, the most famous trailbreaker of them all. And the horses pulling the wagon were stepping out like circus performers on parade, their hides limned by the moonlight so that they seemed bathed in a soft silver fire.

Chapter 8

Flagg led his men deep into desolate country, following a path only he knew. A couple of the horses were skittish, balking at every dark shape, sidestepping clumps of brush and rock outcroppings as if the objects were alive and had teeth and fangs. Some miles from the herd of cattle they had left behind, Flagg reined up and held a hand up to stop the others. When they rode alongside, he finally spoke, in a solemn whisper.

"Right over yonder, beyond that next rise," he said, "is a watering hole. That's where we ought to find some outlaws."

"Outlaws?" Paco said.

"Wild cattle with no brands."

Paco nodded in understanding.

"Now this is dangerous work, boys. And you're going to have to shake out them ropes. I want to go down there and rope at least four head, if we can. Then we'll check for brands. Chase 'em if you have to."

"How many head do you figure are at that watering hole?" Don Horton asked.

"There's always a dozen or so," Flagg said.

"Be hard to rope in the dark like this," Paco Noriega said. He noticed that Flagg, Horton, and Chavez had three or four separate ropes tied to their saddles. He and Mendoza only had one rope apiece.

Flagg looked up, pointed to the nearly full moon. There were a few clouds in the sky, but there were scattered balls of white fluff, and none were near the moon at the moment.

"After we rope some and check for brands, we'll lead those we catch back to the herd, then go to another place for more. We'll be at this all night, boys. Any questions?"

"What's dangerous about it?" Paco asked.

"Some of these steers have been wild for a long time. They'll fight if they're cornered. Those long horns aren't just on their heads for decoration. They can gore you clean through the gut without you ever seeing it coming. Just be careful, all right?"

The others nodded.

"Now," Flagg said, "we'll split up and fan out, circle the watering hole. I'll go in and rope the first one. The others may hold just out of plain curiosity. You all come in fast with your loops built and start snaring cattle like they was catfish in a barrel."

Flagg turned his horse and circled the rise to the left. He motioned for Don and Manny to go to the right. The two young Mexicans followed Flagg, spreading out, watching him closely.

The small pond—what many in that part of the country called a stock tank, or a tank— looked like a rippled mirror in the moonlight. At its edges, dark shapes loomed as indiscernible objects, casting shadows along the edge of the water. There were soft sucking sounds and small splashing noises that drowned out the sawing, high-pitched drone of crickets and the throaty moans of bullfrogs.

Flagg reined his horse to turn it, then prodded its flank with his left spur. The horse, trained to do this, sidled down the slope toward the tank, its hooves falling soft on the ground. Flagg halted the horse when he was about fifteen feet from the edge of the water.

He waited. One cow lifted its head, its curved horns gleaming a velvety black in the moonlight. Flagg swung the rope, letting the loop out, then sailed it toward the set of horns jutting up above the hulks of the other cows. The rope made a low whirring sound and then dropped perfectly over the horns. Flagg jerked out the slack, wound part of rope around his saddle horn, pulled in hard on the reins, and dug in his spurs to both flanks of his horse. The horse backed up, pulling the cow's head sideways until the animal turned and followed the path of least resistance. The other cattle, a dozen or so, looked up, and there was a phalanx of horns silhouetted against the reflective water of the pond. Riders rode in from two directions, swinging their loops overhead. *Swish, swish, swish.* The ropes sailed through the air. One of the lassoed cattle fell down and let out a long mournful groan from deep in its chest. The other cattle scattered, their heads swinging from side to side, heads lowered, horns thrusting.

The pond churned as hooves splashed along the edge. Ripples marred the mirrored surface and frogs leaped into the water with soggy plops. The crickets went silent and the roped cows fought to get free of the loops around their horns, shaking their heads and bucking, kicking their hind legs while in the air.

"Bunch 'em up," Flagg said, dragging his cow toward one that was cavorting like some galvanized being at the end of Horton's rope.

The others rode toward Flagg, pulling their catches behind them.

"Pack 'em close," Flagg said.

Cattle were herd animals and he knew that these would calm down if they could feel their own kind near. When the cows were lined up, he dismounted. His horse backed up, to keep the rope taut, as it had been trained to do. Flagg ran his hands over the rumps of the cows, feeling for brands. He pushed and prodded their rear ends in order to take advantage of the moon and starlight.

"No brands," he said. "Outlaws."

"Those others didn't run far," Horton said. "They're all bunched up yonder starin' down here at us."

"I know," Flagg said. "Tie these up, hobble 'em good, and we'll go after the others. I think they're all part of a wild bunch."

The men worked quickly, securing the cattle so that they could not run away. Then, as Flagg motioned them into a pincer formation, they rode a wide circle around those cows that had escaped. As they drew near from three sides, however, one of the cows bolted and the others quickly followed.

"After 'em," Flagg shouted and the riders streamed after the fleeing cattle, shaking out fresh ropes. Horton and Chavez had given the young Mexicans an extra rope each.

The cattle started to run almost immediately. The riders fanned out as the cattle did and each man tracked down a cow, their horses galloping over the eerie landscape after shadows.

The cows knew every trick. They dodged, backtracked, circled, stood their ground, and then bolted. But, one by one, each rider lassoed the cows they chased and brought them under submission. They all headed back to the cows they had left tied up, where Flagg again checked for brands. None of the cattle had markings on their ears or bodies and he grunted with satisfaction.

"Let's lead these back, then hit another tank," Flagg said. "What we'll do, though, is track to a point ahead of the main herd. Or nearbouts."

"Who will watch them?" Paco asked, as he rode alongside Flagg, leading two cows, as did the others.

"We'll tie 'em up tonight, brand them in the morning when the herd catches up. By then, they will stay with the herd."

"Just hogtie them?" Ricardo wanted to know.

"We'll hobble them. I'll leave one of you to watch over 'em. But we'll wait here for a while, then move slowly. Those cattle that scattered should pick our trail and follow us. We won't even have to rope 'em."

"I hope you have more ropes," Ricardo said.

"Oh, we have plenty of rope, more than you really want, *chamaco*. By morning, you'll never want to see another rope, much less hold one in your hand."

"*No soy chamaco. Soy un hombre*," Ricardo said defensively. "I'm not a boy. I'm a man."

"I know," Flagg said in Spanish. "But you could be one of my sons."

"Do you have sons?"

"Nope. Kids get on my nerves."

After that, Ricardo rode with his friend, Paco, keeping his distance from Flagg.

As Flagg had said, some of the scattered cows began to follow them on their slow course back in the direction of the trail drive. Flagg knew they would stay with the others once he bedded them down for the night.

He decided to leave Horton to watch over those first cows, while he and the others rode back to the chuck wagon to pick up more lariats. The chuck wagon, besides carrying cooking utensils and food, served as a supply wagon, with boxes of horseshoes, nails, extra wood to repair broken wheels, hubs, rope, and medicines. The wagon was, Flagg knew, a necessary component to any long trail drive.

"Let's count head," Flagg said, as he finished hobbling the lead cow. They had brought the cattle next to a small creek, and tied two head to different trees. There were grass and water for the small bunch, and they could be reached later on, in the morning, when it came time to brand the outlaws and shunt them into the main herd.

"See you in the mornin', Jubal," Horton said,

as Flagg and the others rode off to the south for more rope.

"You get some rest, Don. It's going to be like this for a while."

"I know," Horton said, and started building himself a cigarette with the makings in his pocket. He built a small fire to keep warm. It was already turning chilly and midnight was a long way off.

In the far dark, where the moon's light did not stretch, deep in the hardwood canyon called the Palo Duro, coyotes yapped then broke into melodious ribbons of chromatic song—cries that ranged up and down the scale in some ancient cryptic language. Horton listened to them and felt a chill course down his spine. The coyotes seemed to be intoning a kind of death song and death was on his mind that night.

He wriggled his toes in his right boot. He felt the padded oilskin folder with five hundred-dollar bills inside. Deutsch had written out an agreement and had signed it. That was in the packet too. Deuce had given him that money before he left the Rocking D to go with Flagg. It was just a down payment. There were three more packets containing five hundred dollars each waiting for him when he finished the job.

As he smoked, Horton mulled over a way to accomplish his tasks so that they would look like accidents and he would not be suspected.

Deuce wanted him to kill Felix Dagstaff and Jubal Flagg before they reached the Red River. His reward would be two thousand dollars and the deed to Flagg's ranch, which Deuce assured him would be free and clear if Flagg died on the cattle drive north.

The notes of the coyote songs faded away and the moon seemed to glow even brighter as Horton blew a plume of smoke into the air. The smoke floated like a gossamer ghost above his head before the breeze tore it into wisps and the last shred vanished.

Deuce had asked Horton for his loyalty, and he had gladly sworn it to his boss. For the rewards Deuce had promised, a man could be very loyal. Now all he had to do was figure a way to kill two men without arousing any suspicion that he had done it. And he knew, along the Palo Duro, with a large herd of cattle, there would be plenty of opportunities to carry out his deadly mission.

Chapter 9

Dag saw the orange glimmer of a fire along the ragged line of dogwoods. He held up his hand to halt the drive, spoke to the man riding a few yards behind him.

"This is where we stop," Dag said.

The cattle fanned out over the grasslands as dawn was breaking. Off to the left, the hands could see the fire by the creek. They all figured that it meant the end of a long night and the lead rider, Caleb Newcomb, a D Slash hand, flanked the lead cow and started turning the herd to bunch it up and let it water at the creek. Dag looked back at the outriders and signaled for his men to let the herd graze. They had covered nine or ten miles during the night. The men and the stock were tired and hungry.

Little Jake rode up to Dag on the point, met him as he was riding toward the fire and smoke.

"I hope that chuck wagon catches up pretty quick, Mr. Dagstaff," Little Jake said.

"You still got butterflies in your belly, Little Jake?"

"Heck, I got butterflies, moths, crawlin' spiders, and doodlebugs, sir."

"Well, you cracked your cherry last night, son."

"Huh?"

Dag laughed. "Just a joke, Little Jake. Let's see what we got over here. I see cattle by the creek. Must be Flagg's bunch. Go over yonder and holler at Lonnie and tell him to bring the D Slash irons."

"Yes, sir." Little Jake rode off to tell Lonnie Cavins to fetch the branding irons.

Don Horton was puffing on a quirly when Dag rode up. He looked disheveled, red-eyed. The herd around him had swelled, but Flagg was there too, helping the others keep the outlaw cattle from joining the main herd.

"You get a head count?" Dag asked.

"Flagg says we got over forty head," Horton said. "I was catching some shut-eye when he brought in this last bunch."

"Better put some more wood on that fire, Don. We got irons comin'."

Lonnie Cavins carried the D Slash branding irons in his saddlebags. He had four of them in the fire by the time Flagg rode up to talk to Dagstaff.

"You done good, Jubal," Dag said.

"It's a start. There are some more wild cattle just over that hillock there. Followed us in like sheep early this morning."

"How many?"

"Upward of fifty, I reckon. Some folks don't tend their ranches like they should."

Dag let out a low whistle.

"You mean you rounded up over a hundred head last night?"

"At least," Flagg said.

"I'm plumb flabbergasted," Dag said.

"Cows are herd animals. You just got to let them know where the herd ought to go. You got to be slow and patient. But when you're roundin' up outlaws, it works the same. When we run these into the main herd, they'll think they're home for good. It don't take long."

Dag knew that, but he had never seen it work like this. He knew that he had made the right decision in hiring Flagg as trail boss.

The morning sun bleached away most of the shadows and lit the grasses and cacti with a shower of golden light. Dew sparkled like tiny jewels on the plain, and the scent of cactus flowers wafted to Dag's nostrils. The cholla and the nopal were in bloom, the aroma from them heady in the air like some exotic perfume.

The chuck wagon pulled up and stopped nearby a few moments later. Finnerty set the brake as his daughter, Jo, hopped down. He began to set up his cooking irons while Jo cleared ground for a firepit. As he was driving the irons into the ground, she gathered firewood and stacked it next to the place she had cleared. Then she gathered rocks and made a fire ring while her father set up a bench using two sawhorses and a two-by-twelve board. As Jo started the fire, Fingers began mixing flour and water for flapjacks, cracking eggs into the mixture and stirring it with a wooden ladle.

Jo began helping her father after the fire was burning well. She was seemingly oblivious to all that was going on around them. The hands were bulldogging the unbranded outlaw cattle, and four men were pressing hot irons on the hips of the downed cows. The air was filled with the smell of burning hair and flesh. The men grunted and cursed, trying to ignore the smell of food less than a hundred yards away.

Little Jake and Paco led the branded cattle into the main herd, set them to grazing. Caleb Newcomb worked one of the D Slash irons, while Jorge Delgado and Ricardo Mendoza held down the cow to be marked. Dag branded while Ed Langley, another of his hands, and Ricardo Mendoza sat on a squirming steer. Lonnie Cavins branded the cows held down by Chavez and Horton. Flagg and Doofus Wallace kept bringing in a half dozen or so cows at a time, then rode back and rounded up more, dragging some in with ropes, herding those they could.

Fingers held off cooking the flapjacks until all the cows were branded and run into the herd. But he set two large coffeepots with spouts on the fire. Then he started pouring the mix onto large skillets while Jo flipped the flapjacks. There were maple syrup hauled in from Corpus Christi, fried potatoes, and sausage from hogs raised on Finnerty's spread, recently butchered and barreled in brine.

Fingers rang the triangle and the hands who weren't tending the herd streamed over to the chuck wagon like ants to honey. Some of the hands already had empty coffee cups in their hands, the aroma of coffee hung in the air like the delicious taste of chocolate.

Jimmy Gough finished securing the remuda and sauntered over to the group around the chuck wagon and poured himself a cup of coffee.

"Boy," he said, "I can smell the bacon, Fingers. Sugar-cured, I'll bet."

"Just like you, Jimmy," Finnerty cracked.

"How do you keep all them hogs from runnin' off, Fingers?" Wallace, one of the D Slash cowhands, asked.

"You got to know how to build fences, Doofus. Somethin' you cowpokes can't do. That's why you're always chasin' your cattle."

"And how do you build your fences, Fingers?"

"Only one way to build a fence in this country," Finnerty said, "horse high, pig tight and bull strong. I use oak, Doofus, for my fences and for paddles to spank cowboys."

Everyone laughed and Wallace's face turned a pale rose.

Amid the clatter of plates and forks, Jo Finnerty walked over with her plate and sat beside Dag, who had taken one of the planks from the wagon and laid it out over the rocky ground.

"Hello, Dag," she said. "Tired?"

He looked at her. She looked fetching in her colorful calico dress and light sweater, which was blue to match her eyes. She wore a blue ribbon in her hair, as well. Her smile was as warm as the rising sun.

"Yeah, Jo, plumb tuckered."

"We can pull the wagon into the shade and you can sleep underneath."

"I'm not real sleepy. I slept in the saddle some last night."

"Well, suit yourself. I don't want to spoil you."

"Oh, I can be spoiled real easy, Jo."

"Then maybe I will," she said, her voice low and throaty.

Dag thought it had the quality of silk being rubbed by soft hands. He could see why Laura would be jealous of her. She was a beautiful young woman. She kept herself neat and clean and she always smelled like flowers. He could smell her now as she drank her coffee and picked daintily at her plate. But he had known her since pigtails and it was hard now to think of her as a grown woman. Yet she was grown, and he knew she didn't have a beau. They had always been close, but now he knew that something had changed between them. He could no longer sit her on his knee and tousle her hair, or lift her by her arms and swing her around him like a girl on a carousel.

"What was the name of this hog, Fingers?" Lonnie Cavins asked. "It tastes mighty good."

"I don't name no pigs I plan to eat, Lonnie. But if I was to have named this 'un, it might have been Lonnie."

More laughter and the talk among the hands floated around Jo and Dag as they sat together, both of them silent, as if each were wrestling with unspoken thoughts.

"How come you don't keep milk cows, Fingers?" Chad Myers asked.

Finnerty was still making flapjacks, shoveling them onto empty plates. "I keep milk cows. Put the milk in the feed for the hogs every mornin'."

"The trouble with milk cows," Carl Costello said, "is they don't stay milked."

They all laughed at that. Carl had hands that were cracked and blistered. He had milked cows since he was old enough to grasp a teat.

"You ought to know, Carl," Myers said. "I shook hands with him once't and he stripped every dang one of my fingers to see if they had any milk left on 'em."

Jo had scooted closer to Dag so that her leg touched his. Dag didn't notice it at first, but when his leg started to heat up, he knew that she had done it deliberately. No harm in that, he thought. But he felt the pressure and moved his leg slightly. It still burned.

"Felix," she said, "do you remember that time we went fishing in that catfish pond at Daddy's?"

"Yes, I remember it. About five years ago, wasn't it?"

"It was just after a spring rain," she said, "and the banks were muddy."

"And slippery."

She laughed.

"You warned me to be careful, but I didn't listen. I was eager to catch the first fish. We had dug worms on the way there and I grabbed the can away from you."

"You were a scamp, all right, Jo."

"I climbed up on the bank and was about to sit down and put a worm on my hook, when I slid down the smooth bank and fell into the water. I screamed and beat the water. I couldn't swim."

"Yeah. You were quite a sight, Jo."

"You dove in after me and lifted me up in your arms. I fought you because I was scared of drowning, but you got me to the bank and pulled me out. You helped me up to the top and onto dry ground. You held me tight because I was shaking like a leaf."

"I built a fire and you finally dried out."

"I know," she said. "But sometimes, often really, when I'm in bed at night trying to sleep, I can still feel your arms around me, just like they were on that day."

"Jo, you shouldn't talk about these things. Not here. Not right now."

"Why? It's how I feel, Felix."

"I know. But I'm married."

She bit her lip, locking out what she wanted to say. Her hand touched his leg. He looked up at her.

"Don't worry," she said. "I just wanted you to know about that. Because it happened again last night. You were so near, out there with the cattle, yet so far."

"Jo . . . don't."

She took her hand away and sighed.

A few yards away, Horton watched them with narrowed eyes. He sighed too. With satisfaction.

Chapter 10

Flagg took charge shortly after breakfast. He assigned men to ride to places he designated in order to round up more unbranded outlaw cattle. He sent three different groups, one with Horton, another with Mendoza, and a third with Noriega. He sent two men with each leader.

"Those of you going with these men I've put in charge will do what they say. They learned last night how to catch outlaws. You'll go to the watering holes, the outlying tanks, and to shaded places where cattle bed down during the heat of the day. Catch what sleep you can, and bring back some outlaws to brand. We won't be here by the time you get back, so figure out where we'll be by sundown and catch up with us."

The men all nodded and rode off, their saddles dripping with coiled lariats.

He ordered those who stayed behind to sleep for one hour. After that, he said, they would get the herd moving again, at a very slow, grazing pace. He put Manny Chavez in charge of assigning positions for the drive.

"I'll take the point," Flagg told Chavez. "When the herd is moving, you ride drag and take care that none of the cows stray far from the herd."

"I got it, boss," Chavez said.

"Where do you want me, Jubal?" Dag asked.

"You'll take the right flank, ahead of Chavez. Have the remuda and the chuck wagon follow us at a distance of two miles in case we run into anything."

"What anything?" Dag asked.

"Well, maybe Comanch'," Flagg replied, "or Apache."

"We're shorthanded for that sort of shit," Dag said, "until Matlee and his bunch catch up with us."

"When do you expect them?"

"No later than noon. Maybe an hour or so before then."

"We'll stop at high noon for lunch," Flagg said. "Then maybe we can get organized with the Box M boys and add some more outlaws to this herd."

"I saw a lot of wild cattle last year, when I made the trip north," Dag said. "But I expect a lot of 'em are branded by now."

"Dag, there are millions of Mexican cattle in Texas and probably millions still wandering around not carrying brands. We'll fill this herd, by God, and all of us will make a few dollars."

"What about the trail I picked, up the Palo Duro? Do we stand a good chance of making the drive with four thousand head or so?"

"One trail's as good as another, and most side trails lead to the main ones. One thing I've learned since Charlie Goodnight started his trail is that there are as many trails to the railheads as there are ranches in Texas."

Dag laughed. "I believe that."

The herd moved out under a blue sky flocked with little cloud puffs scattered over the heavens like clusters of picked cotton. The herd was surly, but the pace Flagg set that

morning didn't cause any mutiny among them.
When a cow lay down, Flagg told the men to
let it rest until the man riding drag reached it.
Chavez would prod it back on its feet and it
could eat the same dust as he was.

Noon came and there was still no sign of
Matlee. Dag kept watching for telltale dust, but
the back trail was empty, and he felt hollow
inside. He wondered if anything had happened
to Barry. He kept his concerns to himself.

Fingers fed the hands beans and beef, bread
that was already turning hard, peaches served
from the airtights he had brought with him,
and strong coffee. There was little banter during the meal. The men were tired and the cattle
were starting to sprawl out with only three riders making the circuit around the herd. Those
would eat later and by then the herd would be
moving again.

The men who had gone out that morning to
round up outlaw cattle returned, and there was
more branding. This time, Dag and Cavins
used the cookfire to heat the irons. The riders
ate quickly, as Flagg questioned them.

"Any more where these came from?" he asked.

"They're scattered all over," Horton said,
"and they're wild as March hares."

"You brought thirty head," Flagg said.

"We brought thirty-two head," Horton said, correcting him. "I counted them twenty times on the way here."

"You gettin' nervous about somethin', Don?"

"No," Horton said, almost too quickly. "It's just that these were so hard to come by, I didn't want to lose even one head."

"What are you doin' with those wearin' brands?" Flagg asked.

"We've been chasin' 'em well away so they don't foller us back here."

"Well, some showed up, anyways."

"You run 'em off?"

"I didn't recognize the brands. There were Circle T and some Lazy R. A few with notched ears. If the owners come lookin' for them, I'll either give 'em back or buy 'em for the going price."

"Maybe we don't need to check brands so close no more," Horton said.

"Don, when you make your gather, you cut out the branded cows. If some foller you back to the herd, you can't help that none. We'll sort it all out when the time comes."

"I don't hanker to be caught rustlin' another man's cattle," Horton said.

"Well, you ain't, so don't worry about it. Cattle go where they want to go, and on a drive, we can't help what gets mixed in."

"That makes sense," Horton said.

Dag listened to all this without saying anything. After Horton and the others rode off after more wild cattle, he spoke to Flagg.

"Jubal," Dag said, "what do we do about these odd brands when we get to Cheyenne? How do we explain those that aren't Box M or D Slash?"

Flagg rolled a cigarette while Fingers and Jo scrubbed plates with dirt and washed them, put out the fire, and packed up the sawhorses and boards. He lit his cigarette with a lucifer and blew the smoke into the air where the breeze shredded all but the acid aroma.

"If this was a regular roundup, we'd have representatives from all the ranches around us."

"Right," Dag said.

"And if we had time, I could ride to every ranch and offer to buy the head that follered us or just tell the owner to come and pick up his cows."

"That's right, Jubal."

"But we ain't got time to ride a hunnert miles a day lookin' for owners of strays."

"No, we don't."

"So we got some other choices, Dag. We can fill out false bills of sale and hope to hell we don't get caught, or we can use a runnin' iron on them strays and pray to Jesus we don't get caught with the irons or that the buyer finds out what we done."

"Shit, Jubal. We could all get hanged."

"Or just you, Dag."

Jubal pulled on his cigarette and let the smoke dribble out of the side of his mouth.

Dag put a hand to his throat, massaged the flesh as if it were some precious material, which it was.

"I don't much like the idea of that," Dag said.

"There's another thing comes to mind. A couple, really."

"Yeah?"

"First off, when we butcher a beef on the trail, you can bet, by God, that it'll be a cow wearin' a brand what ain't none of ours."

"And the other?"

"We keep a tally at the stockyard in Cheyenne and pay the ranchers when we get back. Adding, maybe, a little profit, but just a little."

"Some might say we took advantage."

"I reckon some might," Flagg said.

Dag looked out at all the cattle. They were moving now, slowly streaming north, in no particular hurry. He was still far short of the number of head he had to have to fill the contract in Cheyenne. Fingers was finished packing the chuck wagon. Jo had gone off to relieve herself and he saw her walking back, patting her hair, straightening her dress. She waved to him and he nodded, still preoccupied with all that he and Flagg had discussed.

"Well, Jubal, what do you reckon I ought to do? We'll have to tell Matlee about the odd brands."

"Yeah, you would. Or just let him find out."

"No, I'm going to tell him straight out."

"That would be my advice."

"So what do we do if Matlee wants those odd brands cut out?"

"Reason with him," Jubal said. "And if he says cut 'em out, we cut 'em out."

"And what happens if we keep all those brands in our herd and we have to explain them to the buyer in Cheyenne?"

"If he's a cattleman, he might look the other way, give you the benefit of the doubt."

"And if he doesn't?"

"Dag, there's some decisions you have to

make on your own. Don't go lookin' for trouble. But if it comes, just meet it head on."

"What would you do, Jubal, if this was your herd?"

"In a way, it is my herd, Dag. I'm responsible for it. What I say goes, on the drive. So I say we keep what we got and cull what we can for vittles along the way, and then let the damned chips fall where they fall."

Jimmy Gough and Little Jake were setting out with the remuda. Dust rose in the air and wafted away like red and brown smoke.

"All right, Jubal. I guess we'll go with what we have. We didn't steal those cattle."

"No, you can't help it if some other man's cattle want to foller you clear across the Red and on up to Cheyenne."

Flagg walked away and climbed aboard his horse. Dag watched him go, then saw Jo climb up onto the wagon seat next to Fingers. She turned and smiled at him. She waved and he waved back.

"See you tonight," she called, as the wagon lurched into motion.

Dag didn't reply. He caught up his horse and stepped into the saddle, but he didn't move. He looked back down the trail from where they had come and scanned the sky. There wasn't a speck of dust, just an emptiness that was like the hollow in the pit of his stomach.

No sign of Matlee and his hands.

Dag tilted his head and marked the passage of the sun in its arc. It was well past noon, well past the time when Matlee should have rejoined the drive.

He turned back and clucked to Nero. He tapped the horse in the flanks with his spurs and they were moving. He passed the chuck wagon and waved without looking at either Jo or Fingers. Then he started circling the tail end of the herd, heading for the right flank.

He felt the weight of all that was on his mind and wondered if he was making the right decision. He couldn't go back now. Deutsch would foreclose on him if he didn't come up with the money to pay off the mortgage and he'd wind up with nothing. Nothing at all.

And now another worry.

Where in hell was Barry Matlee?

Chapter 11

The drive continued along Palo Duro Canyon. Horton and the others brought in small bunches of cattle, but the herd never stopped. Fingers kept a fire going in a large iron bowl, and when it came time for branding, Jo gathered firewood, and Cavins brought out the irons. It was hot and dusty, and the hands rode through rugged country with little water. Finally, by midafternoon, Dag turned in the saddle and saw a cloud of dust to the south. He switched with Chavez and rode drag, falling farther behind as the dust cloud drew closer.

"Jimmy," Dag called, when he could make out the pinpoint silhouettes of riders and horses far to the right, "ride up and tell Jubal to turn the herd in. I think I see Matlee comin'."

Gough stopped the remuda and told Little Jake to hold them up while he rode to the front of the herd.

"Close 'em in, Manny," Dag yelled. "Bunch 'em up. We're going to call a halt for a while."

Chavez started compacting the herd, but he did it slowly and carefully so that the cows wouldn't be alarmed. Gradually, the rear of the herd began to slow even more and the cattle grazed contentedly under the watchful eyes of the outriders.

Several minutes later, Barry Matlee rode up, followed by his hands and their remuda. The cloud of dust thinned and evaporated. The horses were starting to lather, Dag noticed.

"Where in hell have you been, Barry?" Dag pulled his hat off and wiped his sweaty forehead. "You had me plumb worried."

By that time, Flagg was riding up at a gallop, wondering why Dag had sent Jimmy up to call a halt to the drive.

Matlee waited until Flagg joined them before he answered Dag's question. "Hellfire, Dag, that damned Deuce played hob with us right off this mornin'. Wouldn't let us ride acrost his land. I mean he put guns out to stop us doin' what we've always done."

Matlee unleashed his canteen and drank several swallows. His shirt was plastered to his chest with sweat and his face tracked with grime. He looked tired, and so did his men, who were dismounting and leading horses over to Jimmy and the remuda.

"I thought Deuce was going to head out himself," Dag said. "He's taking his sweet time."

"Oh, he's made the gather, all right," Matlee said, as he corked his canteen. Water sloshed in it as Matlee slung it over his saddle horn. "But he and his men blocked us every time we tried to cut a corner or cross a creek that ran across his spread. I mean, those boys were downright belligerent."

"You were threatened?" Flagg asked.

"Yep, his segundo told us he'd shoot the first man who trespassed."

"Any shots fired?" Dag asked.

"Several. Deuce has a bunch of trigger-happy gunmen on his payroll. They shot at the ground, but they shot real close too."

"Son of a bitch," Dag swore. "Well, Deuce is mad that Flagg hired two of his top hands. He's carrying a grudge against me."

"Meanness don't grow overnight," Flagg said. "Deuce was born plumb mean. He's just got himself an excuse now to practice it on y'all."

"It doesn't take a big man to carry a grudge," Dag said. "Deuce is a pretty small man to pull iron on you and your boys, Barry."

"Well, here we are," Matlee said. "Finally. We ain't et nothin' but dust for fifteen miles or better and I feel like I been in a horse stall gettin' kicked to death."

Dag laughed dryly. "Go on up and talk to Fingers, Barry. Maybe he can give you some hardtack and bacon. We're stopped for now, but we'll be movin' on till nearbout nightfall. Right, Jubal?"

"We should make the ground while we can, Dag. This is the easy part. We've got rivers to cross and maybe hostiles waitin' up ahead."

"Oh shit," Matlee said.

Dag stifled a chuckle, but Flagg's face hardened to a bronzed mask.

"This ain't no Sunday buggy ride, Matlee,"

Flagg said. He turned his horse and rode back up to the head of the herd.

"Dag, why in hell did you hire Flagg to be trail boss? He's meaner'n Deuce."

"Wait'll you count head, Barry. Flagg's building our herd as we go."

"How many men has he kilt so far?"

"Take it easy, Barry. Flagg will grow on you."

"Yeah, like a hairshirt."

"You're worn down to a nub, Barry. Go tell Fingers to get you some coffee and vittles. You join up with us when you feel better."

"Yeah, I got me something in my craw, all right: that damned Deuce. And now I got to deal with Jubal Flagg."

Dag let it go. He rode back and relieved Chavez, who took the drag. Dag started the cattle moving, got the ones up that had folded up their legs to rest under the blazing sun. He sighed with something resembling relief.

At least Matlee and his men were now with them. That gave them more strength for the perils they might face in the coming days. He was perturbed that Matlee didn't like Flagg but he understood the other man's feelings. Flagg was not an easy man to like.

The herd roamed on at its slow pace as Horton and the other riders continued to lead or drive stray cattle to the chuck wagon, where Cavins and others branded the unmarked outlaws.

"I'd like to get in on that," Matlee told Dag as they were riding flank together after helping rope and hogtie cattle so that Cavins could mark them with the hot irons.

"What's that?"

"Send some of my hands out to bring in strays."

"Do you have any hands who can beat the brush and bring in thirty or forty head?"

"Sure, Doug Hazlett, Billy Lee Grant, and some others, like Tommy Colgan."

"Better check with Flagg. He took some of my men out and trained them the first night and then those boys taught others how to do an outlaw roundup."

"I'll do that. I notice all the stray ones are wearing D Slash brands. I'd like to see some Box Ms in the herd."

Dag smiled to show Barry that he wasn't trying to cheat him.

"That's how we're going to come up to our quota, Barry. You go right ahead. In fact, if you want, we can just let all the boys we don't need to tend herd go out and split it down the middle."

"Naw, Dag, that wouldn't be right. We'll get our cattle and your boys can get yours."

"Fair enough," Dag said. "I just don't want no fights to break out."

"I'll go talk to Flagg right away," Matlee said.

"Tell him I told you that you can take some of my hands to help the first time out."

Matlee's face darkened as if he had been slapped. "That's all right, Dag. We can manage, I reckon."

"Suit yourself."

Matlee rode off at a canter atop his showy Palomino gelding, Powder.

Dag watched him go and wondered if Flagg had sense enough to make sure the Box M hands went in the opposite direction from where the D Slash boys were bucking the brush. Otherwise, there could be trouble. There were some hot-tempered boys who rode for Barry and he had a few himself. A man's nerves could fray mighty quick under the hot sun when there was close competition. And after all, the cattle were money on the hoof to all of them. He trusted Matlee, but he also knew some of his men might want to cut corners, and way down at the bottom might lie a man's greed. But they had agreed to make the drive to Cheyenne together and keep their cattle separate when the money was paid out. They had shaken hands on it, and he knew Barry was as good as his word. But then, he had never dealt with him when large sums were involved. Money changed everything, he knew.

He hadn't told Barry about the branded cows from other ranches that were running with the herd and all of those he'd watched come in bearing no markings. But it was going to come up, and he had no idea how Matlee would take it. And if it came to the day of the sale, would he be willing to pay the ranchers for the cattle that had mixed in with their herds? He knew he'd have to tell Barry what they were doing before he sent men out to round up outlaw cattle. Otherwise, there'd be hell to pay, maybe.

Flagg didn't like the idea.

"Jubal," Matlee said, "we got one herd here with two separate brands. If my men round up more'n Dag's men do, I don't think it's fair to split even."

"You think your boys can gather more head than we can?"

"What's this 'we,' Jubal? Are you trail boss for me and my boys or just for Dag?"

"I didn't mean it that way, Barry. You know that. You been gone and came late, so I opened the ball with D Slash hands, that's all."

"Well, it sounds to me like Dag wants to hog all the strays for hisself."

"Did he tell you that?" Flagg asked.

"Naw, I don't reckon. I want to ride out tonight and see can we round up some of them outlaws."

Flagg dug in his pocket for a plug of tobacco. He offered it to Matlee, who shook his head. Flagg took that as a sign of impatience. That was why he was trying to slow things down with a chaw. He took his pocketknife and cut off a thumb-sized chunk from the plug and eased it into his mouth. He tongued it into his cheek and began to maul it with his teeth. He didn't speak until he had spit a stream of brown juice at a colony of ants swarming over their little sandy hill.

"You might find slim pickin's along this

stretch of the Palo Duro," Flagg said, "though I ain't sayin' you will. There's so many cattle roamin' around Texas, no tellin' where they all are. It's just that I've been lookin' all day and ain't seen none. You might want to get acquainted with the country a little first before you take your men out on a wild-goose chase."

"Damn it, Jubal. You sound discouragin'," Matlee said.

Flagg chewed and Flagg spat.

"Ain't that way at all. But you just rode up on us and haven't even had time to pick yourself a wildflower. Wait a day or so. Then you can take to the brush."

"I ain't waitin', Jubal. I just want you to make sure we don't run into D Slash riders wherever we decide to go."

"You want me to point you somewheres like I did with Dag's boys."

"That's right."

"You don't need to get your dander up about it, Barry. I can do that. I will do that. You just tell me when."

"Tonight."

"Moon's on the wane now," Flagg said.

"Damn you, Jubal. You sure as hell are buckin' me."

"Tonight, Barry. Right after supper. Now go someplace and cool off. You got a hot collar and it ain't from the sun."

Matlee snorted and rode off.

Flagg watched him go and shook his head. He spit a stream of tobacco juice in Matlee's direction, although he was a good two hundred yards away.

"Trouble," Flagg said to his horse. "It comes whether you expect it or not."

Then he turned back to the way ahead, looking for a line of trees that would mark a creek where they could stop for supper, at least.

He thought that he might just run the herd all night to give those Box M boys a good sweat.

Chapter 12

There was little water that night. Flagg didn't find a creek, but he found some depressions that had collected water from the last rain and that was where he ordered the men to bed the cattle down for the night.

He had come to another decision as well.

Flagg gestured to Dagstaff, as the hands who were not tending to the herd gathered to smoke and talk and wait for supper. The two men walked out of earshot of the others. Flagg chewed on a cud of tobacco, his face as dusty as the land itself, his eyes peering out of sweat-soaked mud holes.

"Dag, I'm going to turn Matlee and his bunch out tonight to round up strays he can put his Box M brand on. We'll keep your boys in camp. Let 'em get some shut-eye."

"That's fine with me, Jubal. But there's something else behind it, ain't there?"

"Maybe. Let Barry get his feet wet."

"I hope he finds a passel of outlaws."

"He won't."

"We're not in competition, Jubal."

"I'm not so sure, Felix."

Dag looked over, saw that Matlee was glaring at them from where he was leaning against one of the wagon wheels, rolling a quirly. He couldn't make out the expression on Barry's face, but he could imagine what he was thinking.

"I ain't gonna ride that road with Matlee, Jubal."

"Good. Maybe we can have a peaceful journey."

"We by God better."

The two men left it at that. They split up and walked their separate ways. As Dag approached the chuck wagon, he felt Matlee's gaze on him. The coffee was boiling. He got a cup off the wagon, walked to the fire, picked up the pot, and poured some in his cup.

Finnerty had driven his cooking irons into the ground and a pot full of stew hung over the fire, its blackened bottom licked by lashing flames.

Dag turned and saw Jo standing there, a smile curving her lips.

"Don't spill that on me," she said lightly.

"Jo, I'll get out of your way."

"Will we be here for the night?"

"Yes, we all need some rest."

"Good. I think I found a catfish pond. I've got some poles in the wagon."

"You want to go fishing, Jo?"

"I thought it would be nice. A change."

He stepped to her side, away from the fire. He tipped the coffee cup to his lips.

"Early?" he asked. "Late?"

"When it turns cool."

"We don't have any worms."

"I've got some liver. Pa butchered a cow today and I saved some. It won't last and it makes good bait."

"We'll do 'er," Dag said. "Wanta bet?"

"First fish? Biggest?" She laughed.

"First."

"A nickel."

"A nickel."

She smiled at him and he walked behind the wagon, where he could watch the setting sun.

He took a deep breath, wondering if he had made the right decision. It was harmless enough, he decided. He and Jo had fished many times before. But not out there, not in that vast emptiness, that long plain that stretched from every horizon in every direction.

Nothing will happen, he told himself. *We'll fish and we'll swap stories. Like always.*

Then, after another sip of coffee, he quietly said something else. "Felix, you're a damned fool."

Horton and the other cowhands rode in with a half dozen head of cows to show for a long day's work. The sun was setting and the men looked tired. Cavins and Jorge Delgado made short work of the branding and the cattle were turned into the herd. Flagg handed out assignments to the nighthawks, with Dagstaff standing by. He saw Matlee looking at him and he nodded.

"Don," Flagg said, "you and your boys can rest up tonight. I'm sending Matlee and his hands out ahead of us to rustle the brush for outlaws."

"They won't find nary a cow for twenty mile," Horton said.

"Maybe they will and maybe they won't, Don. But they'll get their cherries busted."

Everyone laughed, including Jo. She rang the dinner triangle with a ladle and the men lined up for supper as the sun sank below the western horizon, leaving a soft orange glow in the sky.

After supper, Matlee divided up some of his hands and directed them to go to different locations ahead of where the herd was bedded down. Those of the D Slash outfit who had been out before offered plenty of advice, mostly in the form of wisecracks.

"Don't wear red. Them outlaws can see in the dark."

"If you get off your horse, you better be wearin' horn-proof clothes."

"Ropin' cows in the dark is like bein' in a coal mine. You don't know what you're goin' to catch."

And then the Box M boys rode out under the slender moon, disappearing into the darkness. The cattle lowed and moaned as the men passed the herd, and the nighthawks waved them on, wishing them good luck.

"Well, there they go, Jubal." Dag heaved a sigh.

"Did you talk to Barry about bringing back branded cattle?"

"No, I never had the chance. He'll find out soon enough."

"That man's already got a burr under his saddle, I'm thinkin'."

"We'll just have to see what he brings in," Dag said.

"If he brings in anything." Flagg spit a gob of tobacco and juice, then slapped his leg with the flat of his hand. "I'm goin' to turn in, Dag. Looks clear tonight. The herd's settled down some, and unless somethin' spooks 'em, they should be quiet."

"You're not thinkin' stampede, are you, Jubal?"

"Not tonight, anyways. You get a herd this size and one nervous cow—hell, anything can happen."

"Now you're makin' me nervous."

"Well, don't snore too loud tonight, Dag."

Dag walked over to the chuck wagon. Finnerty and Jo were finished with the dishes. Jo was getting a couple of cane poles out of the wagon, along with some string, a sack of hooks and weights, and a package of bloody liver in a tin can. She was wearing the same calico dress, but had donned a light wool shirt. He had seen her in overalls back home, but she knew a lot of the hands didn't like women in men's pants, so he had told her not to wear overalls or trousers on the drive.

"Is your daddy comin' with us, Jo?" Dag asked.

"No. You know better than that, Felix. Daddy doesn't like to fish."

"He doesn't like to eat them either, does he?"

She laughed and handed him a pole and the can with the liver in it.

"How far is this catfish pond?" he asked, as they started out.

"Not far. Maybe two miles. I rode Sugarfoot out there after we stopped."

"We'll walk it, then."

"Yes, it's such a nice evening."

As the two started out, Don Horton emerged out of the darkness. "Where you goin', Dag?" he asked.

Dag held up his pole. "What do you think this is, Don? A lightning rod?"

Horton laughed.

"Miss Jo, good evenin'," Horton said. "Is Dag takin' you snipe huntin'?"

"I'll bet you know all about snipe hunting, Mr. Horton."

"Snipe hunting" was a trick older boys played on younger boys. They took a boy out in the woods with a gunny sack and made the boy stand there with the empty sack, saying they would drive the snipes to him. Then the big boys just left him there, wondering how long it would take the younger lad to figure it all out. Jo had been taken snipe hunting herself.

"Well, I know there ain't no fish in any of them muddy tanks," Horton said.

"Well, I found a spring-fed pond that does have fish in it. Good evening, Mr. Horton."

Dag chuckled and they kept walking.

When they were out of earshot, Jo whispered, "I'm glad you're wearing a six-gun, Felix."

"Why? I always wear it when I'm working or out after dark."

"I know. Don Horton gives me a funny feeling, that's all. I don't know why he was teasing us."

"It's just his way," Dag said.

"He knew where we were going. He heard me ask you."

"He did?"

"I've been watching that man, Felix. And he's been watching you."

"What?"

"Whenever you're not looking, he's watching you, like a cat watches a mouse—or like a hawk sitting on a fence post looking at a rabbit."

Dag laughed, but it wasn't much of a laugh, more of a snort of disbelief. "Don and I don't have no bad feelin's between us, far as I know," he said.

"Then I wonder why he keeps watching you like a red-tailed hawk."

Dag shrugged. "Maybe he finds me interestin'," he joked.

"Just don't turn your back on him when you're off by yourself. He might just be behind you."

Jo said no more about it. Dag made a note to himself that he'd keep a closer eye on Horton, but he had no idea why the man would be watching him. Maybe it was just Jo's imagination.

"Here's the pond," she said.

The water shimmered in the faint moonlight. It had high banks like the pond he had at home. Someone had widened it with shovels and there were tracks around it from deer, cattle, and coyote. Someone had tended it, so there ought to be cattle around close. He wondered why Horton had found so few.

"You can see it bubbling over on one end," she said. "There's a spring under here, and I saw fish when I rode up here this afternoon."

"Did the fish have whiskers?"

She laughed. "Let's find out."

They sat on the bank and rigged their poles with line, hooks, and sinkers. Dag cut up the liver into small chunks and they baited their hooks.

Jo threw her line in the water. The sinker made a splash and then sank, dragging the line with it. Dag put his line in a moment later.

"You got a head start on me, Jo," he chided.

"First fish."

Dag chuckled. "A bet's a bet," he said.

All of a sudden, Jo pulled back on her pole and reared backward. Her line was taught and was making circles as it cut the water.

"I got one!" she exclaimed and bent back even farther, pulling on the line to keep out the slack.

That move probably saved her life, because just then, a rifle shot cracked. Dag heard a bullet sizzle just past his ear, frying the empty air where Jo had been a second before.

Dag's blood froze as his belly knotted in fear.

Chapter 13

Dag lunged to cover Jo with his own body, smothering her under his weight. The sound of the gunshot lingered in his ears for several seconds. And then it grew quiet. He thought he heard the sound of running footsteps, but he couldn't be sure.

Jo struggled to free herself, squirming beneath Dag.

"Hold still," he whispered. "Listen."

Jo stopped struggling. They both listened, but all they heard was the sound of crickets sizzling in the grasses surrounding the pond, and the throaty wharrumping of the bullfrogs.

They listened some more, turning their heads so they didn't hear their own breathing.

The cattle were quiet, except for a few still roaming around. The occasional *whuff* of a horse clearing its nostrils sounded. A far-off coyote yodeled. The distant whirruping call of a whip-poor-will was answered by another even farther away. Underneath all the vagrant sounds was the soft susurrance of their breathing, and underneath that lay the deathly silence of a graveyard at midnight.

"Felix," Jo whispered.

"Yeah?"

"I don't hear anything."

"No, not anymore."

"What happened?"

"Someone took a shot at us."

"I heard it," she said. "Who? Why?"

"It wasn't a ricochet. I mean it was a straight shot. Aimed at you. Or me."

She shuddered beneath him.

He looked down at her, her face barely visible in the moonlight, but the contours all there, the nose shadowed, the lips. Invisible eyes in dark sockets.

He slid from Jo's body and lay beside her, still listening.

Something moved. Dag saw that Jo's hand

was wiggling. She still clutched the pole with the dancing fish on the end of her line.

"I caught a fish," she said. "He's still on."

"Well, throw him back in."

"But I won," she said, her voice a teasing whisper in his ear.

"Yeah, Jo, you won. Let's get out of here and back to camp. We'll see who's up, who's pretending to be asleep."

"What if he's still out there, waiting for us?"

"We're going to make a wide circle," he said, "go back a different way than the way we came."

Dag got up, drew his pistol. He peered into the darkness, looking for any movement, any sign of life across the empty plain. There was nothing that he could see.

Jo got up, brushed herself off. She still held the pole in one hand. She crept up the bank on all fours and squatted. She pulled on the line, bending her pole back over her shoulders. There was a splash, and the inertia gone, she fell backward, stopping herself just before she tumbled down the bank.

"Oh, it got away," she said, still in a whisper.

"Good. Now I don't have to pay you that nickel. Let's get the hell out of here. Just follow me, Jo."

He picked up his pole and helped Jo down the bank. They walked away from the pond, keeping it between them and the direction where they heard the rifle shot. Dag held his pistol at the ready, but it was uncocked.

"Where are we going?" she asked.

"We'll come up on the herd from the south," he said. "Maybe add another half mile to a mile to our walk out here."

She was silent for a few moments. "Felix," she whispered, moving close enough to him that their bodies touched, "I can still feel you on me."

"Huh?"

"Back there. When you were lying on top of me. Protecting me. I liked it. I felt safe."

"Ain't no nothin' in that, Jo."

"Yes, there is," she said, her whisper louder than before. "There are feelings. My feelings. Yours, maybe."

"I just didn't want you to get shot is all." His voice was gruff as if he were not at all certain that what he said was true.

"I know. You were protecting me, Felix. But

it was nice having you so near. Almost as if . . ."

"As if what?"

"As if we were married."

Dag swallowed hard. There it was, he thought. Jo did have her eyes on him. As Laura had said.

"Jo, we're not married. I am married. To Laura. That's not going to change."

"I know," she said quickly. "But a girl can dream, can't she?"

"Maybe you should learn to be more realistic, Jo."

"I've loved you for a long time, Felix. I will always love you. I can't help that."

"Maybe not. But you shouldn't talk about marriage with a married man, that's all."

"All right. I won't. I promise. I just wanted you to know how I felt about you, Felix."

"You'll make some man a good wife someday, Jo. That's what you should be thinking about."

She flung her head back in defiance, but said nothing.

As they drew close to camp, Dag saw that there was a lot of riders circling the herd. He heard one of the men singing softly. Some of the cattle were on their feet. The cattle were lowing and he could feel that they were restless, ready to bolt at the first loud noise or follow the first panicked cow. His heart felt as if it were sinking.

"That shot must have made the herd jumpy," he said. "Come on, let's see what's going on."

He started to trot and Jo kept up with him. They reached the chuck wagon and Dag handed her his fishing pole. He holstered his pistol and started looking for Flagg.

Flagg was riding toward him. He appeared out of the darkness and Dag waved to him. Flagg rode up, swung down out of the saddle.

"Where in hell have you been, Dag?"

"Jo and I were fishing."

"Well, some jackass shot at a coyote and liked to spook the whole damned herd."

"Do you know who fired the shot?"

"Did you hear it where you were?"

Dag decided not to tell him that he and Jo had been shot at.

"Yeah, we heard it."

"Wasn't you, was it?"

"Are you crazy, Jubal? I wouldn't do anything like that."

"I didn't think so. But it's damned funny. Only it ain't funny. I'd like to get my hands on the jackass who shot off the gun."

"What makes you think someone was shooting at a coyote?"

"I seen Don cleaning his rifle and asked him if he knew who had fired the rifle."

"And what did Don say?" Dag's voice was level, his tone guarded.

"He said he heard someone say there was a coyote after the herd."

"Who?"

"He didn't say, didn't know."

"Well, coyotes aren't going to run in on a big herd. Not just one coyote anyway."

"That's what I thought. A damned fool thing to do, whoever done it."

Dag let it go. He walked back to the chuck wagon and said good night to Jo. Then he got his bedroll from his saddle. He walked over to where Jimmy and Little Jake had their bedrolls and laid his out. There was no sign of Horton, the bastard.

With the herd calmed down, all the hands not on watch returned and took to their kips. Little Jake and Jimmy crawled into theirs.

"You awake, Dag?" Jimmy asked.

"Just barely. Why?"

"You missed all the fun."

"I miss a lot some days."

"Well, g'night."

"Night, Jimmy."

Dag slept with his pistol close at hand. He dreamed of deep canyons and fish swimming in dark pools. He dreamed of faceless men chasing him and dead-end rides through empty towns from which there was no escape. And he dreamed of Jo and Laura and of someone trying to tear them both away from him.

Flagg got the herd moving at sunup, and when Matlee and his men returned, shortly afterward, they had no cattle with them. Matlee was in a bad mood and griped about missing breakfast, but Finnerty fed his men hardtack and cold bacon, which he had saved for them. The Box M hands ate on horseback and slept in their saddles as the sun came up, hot and bright, burning off the dew and making men and horses start to sweat.

They made fifteen miles that day and the land began to change in subtle ways. Dag supposed that was just an illusion, because the color and the growing things looked pretty much the same. But it seemed to open up and widen as if they had ridden into another country, and when he looked at Palo Duro Canyon, it was red with streaks of gray and brown. Birds flitted in the brush and lizards sunned themselves on rocks. A hawk floated over the canyon, sailing on silent pinions, its wings spread wide, its head turning from side to side, soaring on invisible currents of air.

The next day, Flagg sent a rider out ahead of the herd and Dag asked him why.

"I thought I saw smoke this morning," Flagg said.

"Smoke?"

"Not regular smoke. Signal smoke. Way off. I couldn't be sure."

"Comanches?"

"That's what I figure. I sent Caleb Newcomb up ahead to scout it out."

"Did you see one smoke or two?"

"I thought I saw two."

"Could be," Dag said, "but Comanches use mirrors these days. I haven't seen signal smoke since I was a kid."

"These were way far apart," Flagg said.

"Mirrors go a long ways, Jubal."

"See them clouds up ahead?"

Dag stood up in the stirrups and shaded his

eyes. There were fat, fluffy clouds ahead, huge thunderheads cascading to higher altitudes. When he glanced up at the sky above him, he saw that there were clouds all around. He looked down and saw shadows on the ground.

"Ain't no sun yonder," Flagg said.

"Maybe you just saw clouds," Dag said.

"Could be. Won't hurt Caleb none to stretch his legs on a fine day such as this."

"Nope. You're the boss."

Dag wondered where Horton was. He had not seen him that morning. He got the feeling the man was avoiding him. Dag hadn't seen him, in fact, since the night when someone shot at him. He wanted to see Horton. He wanted to look him in the eye and see if Horton avoided his gaze. That would tell him something, he reasoned.

Caleb rode up fast, his hat brim flattened, his horse eating up ground.

"Mr. Flagg," he said when he reined up, "I sure as hell seen something."

"Yeah, Caleb, what'd you see? Injuns?"

"No, sir. But you got to come look. I don't know what to make of it. I ain't never seen nothin' like it."

"Caleb, I got better things . . ." Flagg started to say.

But Caleb had turned his horse and was riding back from where he had just come from as if he were being chased by the devil himself.

Chapter 14

Caleb Newcomb finally reined in his horse after the shouts from Jubal and Felix reached his ears and sank in. But he didn't stop, only slowed his mount to a fast, butt-pounding walk until the trail boss and rancher could catch up to him.

"What the hell, Caleb?" Flagg roared. "You tryin' to kill that horse right from under you?"

"You gotta see," Caleb said. "There, just over that rise." He pointed to a point on the horizon some five hundred yards ahead of them.

"Remember this, Dag?" Flagg asked.

"No, I rode t'other side of Palo Duro. What is it?"

"It don't look good," Flagg said. "We must be a mite off track."

Caleb waited for them as they rode up the rise. They all heard a far-off, high-pitched whistle. Then the three riders cleared the top of the rise.

Dag saw them. The air was filled with those same piercing whistles and then they were gone.

"Damned prairie dogs," Dag said.

"Ain't just that," Flagg said. "That's a prairie dog town. Biggest I ever saw."

Caleb found his voice, finally. "I never saw such a sight," he said. "Far as you can see. I come up on 'em and them whistles spooked my horse. He reared up and whinnied to beat hell. I near fell off. One minute they was hundreds of them standin' like statues and then they all went into the ground and it got so quiet I wondered if I was dreamin'."

"Not hundreds," Flagg said, surveying the little piles of dirt in every direction. "Millions."

"We'll have to go around," Dag said. "Don't you think, Jubal?"

Flagg didn't say anything for several moments. Instead, he looked across the vast expanse of plain that was dotted with dirt

mounds thrown up by the prairie dogs when
they dug their intricate network of tunnels un-
derground. Then he looked off to the west, to
the gorge that was Palo Duro Canyon, with its
steep sheer walls. He had been in the canyon
before, had marveled at its bright bands of layered colors: yellow, brown, orange, red, ma-
roon, gray, and white.

He had seen fossilized imprints of long-
extinct animals and plants embedded in the
rocks, and he knew the canyon had good grass
growing between the majestic pinnacles, buttes,
and mesas, each layered over and protected by
sandstone or other kinds of rock that protected
the outcroppings from erosion. The floor of the
canyon was dotted with several kinds of good
grasses, as well as nopal, the prickly pear cactus, yucca, mesquite and juniper. It would be
treacherous to drive the herd through there,
but it might cost them several head of cattle
and perhaps some horses if they tried to cross
the prairie dog town with its treacherous holes
that could snap an animal's leg like a twig at
any misstep.

"Dag, we've got to turn the cattle into the
canyon," Flagg said.

"How in hell do we get down there?"

"We'll have to find a place where the land is eroded, a small pass through where we can herd 'em in."

"All right. Let's start lookin' before that herd catches up with us."

Flagg turned to Newcomb. "Caleb, you ride back and tell Manny Chavez to slow down the herd until we get back there."

"You want him to stop the drive?" Newcomb asked.

"Just slow 'em down some. Now wear out some leather, son."

Caleb rode off, whipping his horse with the ends of his reins and digging spurs into its flanks.

"I swear," Flagg said, "he'll founder that horse if he don't have sense enough to grab another'n out of the remuda."

Dag was already turning his horse toward the canyon, nearly two miles distant.

"When we get there," Flagg said, "we'll split up. You go south and I'll go north."

"Watch out for prairie dog holes," Dag said.

And that was what they did, weaving their way in and out of the maze of earth mounds marking the dangerous holes. At the canyon's edge, both men reined up. They each looked both ways, north and south.

"I don't see anything right close," Dag said.

"You holler if you find a break, Dag."

Dag turned left to the south and Flagg rode in the opposite direction.

He did not have to ride far. He turned and saw that Flagg had not gone far either.

"Jubal, down here," Dag called. "I found a place."

Flagg turned his horse and headed back toward Dagstaff. Dag rode up to the place he had spotted. It appeared to be a long playa where dozens of flash floods had washed a fissure in the canyon walls. Perhaps a hundred yards wide, it sloped down into the canyon. He saw something else too, and it made his blood turn to ice in his veins. Dag waited for Jubal.

"That's a good spot," Flagg said. "Wide enough, I think. We'll just funnel the cattle down there and drive on past that prairie dog town and hope to hell we can find a place along the wall where we can get 'em up on top again."

"Jubal, look at those tracks."

Dag pointed and Flagg sat up straight in his saddle as if he had been struck by a wet mop across his face.

"Be damned," he said.

"Unshod pony tracks," Dag said, "and cow tracks. Maybe that same bunch of Comanches that ran off some of my cattle."

"Comanches or Kiowas or Apaches maybe," Flagg said.

"I don't like it none," Dag said.

"We get down in that canyon and we'll be sitting ducks for Injuns up on the rim."

"So what are we going to do, Jubal?"

"Ain't got no choice. I see there's plenty of grass down there and water running beyond that little butte. See it?"

Dag looked and saw a flashing ribbon of silver in the sunlight, just beyond a small butte. And there was plenty of grass. There might be something else down there too: Comanches or Kiowas or Apaches—maybe all three kinds of Indians.

"I see it," Dag said. "All right, we'll send scouts ahead of us once we get the herd down there, if you agree."

"I agree. You wait here and look things over, Dag. I'll ride back and turn the herd. This is a good place and the cattle don't have to cross any prairie dog holes." Flagg turned his horse and rode off to the east.

When he was gone, Dagstaff felt very alone. But was he? He looked all around and listened. Only the sound of the wind sighing down the canyon. Palo Duro. The Spaniards had named it. It meant "hardwood," and there were hardwoods in it—and cactus, lizards, rattlesnakes, armadillos, and roadrunners.

He rode down the playa into the canyon, marveling at the exquisite beauty, with all the striated colors along the canyon walls, the greenery. It was like riding into an oasis, into a secluded paradise that was almost magical. It fair took his breath away.

He rode past the small butte and looked at the stream. It was sluggish but moving. He wondered how far up it ran and when it would peter out. *Be hell to get caught down here*, he thought, *if a big storm came up and rained into it. A flash flood in the canyon would wash away and drown everything in its brutal path.*

The pony tracks led north, up the canyon toward Amarillo—or toward a Comanche camp. He knew the Indians camped down in it and had heard tales of how well they could hide and fight off soldiers or rangers who went down there to hunt them. It gave him the willies to think that he was down here and everything so quiet, so innocent-looking.

The canyon, at that place, was four or five miles wide and there was a bend to the north, where it narrowed some. Maybe, he thought, they were avoiding one danger with the prairie dog holes and riding right into an even greater one.

Dag knew he was in an ancient world, and it was haunting, as if he had dreamed it all once, long ago. In the rock layers, he saw ages past, dirt piled upon dirt, rock upon rock, and the weather, over time, had sculpted the canyon and hidden it below the plain as if God had wanted to shield its beauty from all but the bravest and hardiest. It looked old and it smelled old, even with the new grasses and flowers of spring, the blossoms on the nopal, the delicate wires of the cholla, and the stately yucca with its pale yellow adornments. He heard a quail pipe in the distance and saw it sitting atop a yucca, warning its flock, a lone sentinel with a long view from its perch on the tallest plant.

There were deer tracks and coyote tracks and

the heavy track of a wolf. A lizard splayed itself on a rock that caught the sun, the rays warming its cold blood. Its eyes blinked at Dag and its head moved slightly, a quick motion that suddenly froze. Snake tracks crossed the playa, then disappeared among the rocks.

Dag drew a deep breath and wondered how long he dared linger in that solemn old place, where the breeze whispered secrets in a language he could not understand. The raw beauty of the place was intoxicating and he knew the real danger was that a man might go down into it and never return, never want to return.

Dag turned his horse and rode back up the playa to the world he knew, the vast plain stretching as far as the eye could see. He rolled a cigarette, lit it, and let the smoke warm his throat and burn his lungs. There was peace here too, but it was another world, wide-open, as big as the blue sky above him. He could see a long way there, but he knew he could not see as much.

After a time, he heard the lowing of cattle, the growls of thirsty animals that could not yet smell water. He looked to the south and saw Flagg waving to him; behind Flagg, the herd streamed at a brisk lope, with cowhands yelling at them, waving their hats at the slow ones and at the ones that drifted away from the herd.

Dag had long since finished his cigarette, but the tobacco taste still lingered. He rode toward Flagg and saw Caleb Newcomb and Manny Chavez riding behind the other man, turned the herd toward the opening in the canyon.

"Like the boy rabbit said to the little girl rabbit, Felix," Flagg said, " 'This won't take long.' "

Dag laughed. "You got here right quick. Them cattle are plumb parched."

"Well, they'll have water and I can send out scouts once we have 'em down in the canyon. You go in there?"

"Yes."

"See anything?"

Dag took a breath. "Naw," he said. "I didn't see a damned thing. It's pretty quiet, so far."

Flagg looked at him in disbelief, but let it go. He had seen that same look on the face of a man watching a burning sunset or a fiery dawn and, sometimes, in a church when the spirit gripped a man clean down to his socks.

Some things, he knew, a man kept to himself.

Chapter 15

The thunderheads had drifted away by late afternoon, when the last of the herd filed down into the canyon. And there wasn't much shade in the canyon. The cattle had been watered, and they were grazing north up through the wide and winding wonderland that was the Palo Duro. Flagg sent riders ahead and one to ride the eastern rim, three men in all. They had been gone for some time and Dag had ridden back and forth along the line of cattle, which now numbered more than fifteen hundred head. He knew that Flagg had sent Jorge Delgado and Little Jake Bogel to ride point, while Ed Langley rode the rim.

Matlee was not there, nor were any of his

men, which irritated Dag. But something else irritated him even more. He kept looking for the man, but he had not seen him all afternoon. And it began to worry him. Finally, he rode up to Flagg at the head of the driven herd and asked him, flat-out, "I don't see Don Horton anywhere, Jubal. Did he drift off or desert?"

Flagg chuckled. "No, I sent him off with Barry Matlee."

"How come?"

"Well, you heard Matlee at breakfast. He said he was going outlawin' and wouldn't come back until he had at least a hunnert head to drive back."

"So?"

"So, after that, Don came up and said he'd like to ride with Matlee, maybe show him some old cowhand tricks."

"Well, if we run into anything serious, Jubal, we're sure as hell short of men."

Flagg turned his horse and halted him, looking Dag square in the face. "You don't like the way I run this outfit, Dag?"

"Hey, hold on, Jubal. No need to get your dander up, son. I'm just nervous, is all. Has nothin' to do with the way you ramrod."

"Just so we're clear on that, Dag."

"Christ, you're touchy, Jubal."

"It's turnin' to a long day, Dag. You better ride back up the rim where we come in and look for the chuck wagon."

"You tell Fingers where we were headed?"

"Didn't have time. But I'm thinkin' we'd best keep him and the wagon up on the flat. It's mighty rugged and uneven ground down here."

"That's so. And it might be hell getting it out of here, especially if a flash flood was to come roarin' down the gorge."

"I've noticed a lot of game trails streaming down off the flat, on both sides, so I'm thinkin' I'll draw up the herd come this evenin' where the men can ride or walk up one of them trails and get their grub."

"Yeah, that's a good idea, Jubal."

"See? I do know what the hell I'm doin', sometimes."

"Let's not be scratchin' that itch no more, Jubal."

"Fair enough, Dag."

Jubal clucked to his horse and nudged its flanks with his spurs. Dag turned his horse and rode to the edge of the canyon wall, where he could retrace his steps and get back up on the flat. Fingers would wonder where in the hell everyone went, and it would be bad if he rode into that prairie dog town.

Dag headed up the playa to the plain and went two miles, to where the old cattle trail would have been, had they driven straight to the prairie dog town. He stopped Nero and the horse blew its nostrils and began to graze while Dag looked to the south. He saw the single large speck on the horizon and stood up in the stirrups and waved his hat. Then he sat back down in the saddle and waited, watching as the speck grew larger, then dissolved into several separate specks. He stood up, straight-legged, in the stirrups, held on to the horn, and waved his hat again. This time, two men waved hats back and he knew it was Jimmy and Little Jake bringing on the remuda. Dust smudged the sky above the horse herd, the haze shimmering rust and brown in the glow of the sunlight.

Off to the left of the remuda, Dag saw another speck, but larger. He knew that was the chuck wagon, flanking the sixty-odd horses, and it was raising dust of its own. Dag tautened the reins and ticked Nero's flanks with his spurs and rode off toward Jimmy and Little Jake.

"Boy, we must be a-ways behind that cattle herd," Jimmy said. "I ain't seen no dust since we topped that last rise. We had some trouble with a couple of the horses. It was turning into a prizefight and they had to break it up and separate 'em. What brings you out this way, Dag? Didn't run into anything harder than a rock, did you?"

Jimmy was sweating and his light shirt looked almost black.

Dag turned Nero and rode alongside him. "There's a dog town up yonder, Jimmy. So you can turn your remuda to the west. 'Bout two miles away, there's Palo Duro and the herd's down in the canyon."

"Be damned," Jimmy said.

"You'll find a playa where a flash flood opened up a path into the canyon. Just run 'em down there and you can't get lost less'n these nags can climb walls straight up"

"Dag, don't you be talkin' about these fine breeds that way."

Both men laughed.

Jimmy turned to Little Jake on the other side of the herd and yelled at him.

"We'll turn 'em here and head west, Little Jake. Look lively, son."

Little Jake grinned. The two men smiled at each other.

"I'll catch up to you by and by, Jimmy. I'm going to talk to Fingers and bring him over next to the canyon."

"You takin' the wagon down in there?"

Dag shook his head. "Nope. Just going to ride shotgun for Fingers along the top edge of the rim. We'll likely see you round suppertime."

"You ride careful, Dag," Jimmy said. He touched a finger of farewell to the brim of his battered felt hat, which had a dark band of sweat around the lower part of the crown, where the moisture had dropped through. The band was caked with dust.

Dag turned his horse and rode toward the chuck wagon, which was looming ever larger as it approached.

Jo was the first to wave from the seat of the wagon. Her father waved when Dag was still some distance away. He felt a trip hammer rhythm in the region of his heart when Jo waved. It surprised him because he had not been thinking of her in any special way. But there were flutters in his stomach and his pulse raced. She was a beautiful young woman, of course, but that didn't explain his reaction to seeing her. No, there was something else beneath it. She stirred feelings in him that had long been dormant. He would have to watch himself, he vowed silently, as he rode up to the wagon.

"Somethin' up, Dag?" Finnerty said as Dag rode alongside.

"We're drivin' the herd up the Palo Duro, Fingers, but there's a prairie dog town like you never saw up ahead and you'll have to turn west to keep out of the worst part."

"Big town?"

"Huge."

"We goin' into the canyon?"

"Nope. Might not get out. And if a flash flood happens down in there, you'd turn this wagon into a rowboat."

Finnerty laughed.

"It's good to see you, Felix," Jo said. "Are you going to escort us?"

"Yes'm," Dag said, and mentally kicked himself for being so formal with a girl he'd known for most her life.

Jo frowned.

"Am I a 'ma'am' now, Felix?"

"No'm—I mean, naw, Jo, I just—"

"Just what?" she teased.

Finnerty looked at both of them and smiled. "You just got your tongue all tangled up, didn't you, Dag?"

"I reckon," Dag said lamely.

"Daddy, Felix can speak for himself."

"I know that, darlin'. I'm just trying to make the man more comfortable, is all. You bat them pretty eyes of yours at men and they lose their senses."

"Oh, Daddy, stop it."

When Dag didn't say anything and she could see that he was feeling somewhat uncomfortable, she turned to her father. "Daddy, tell Felix about what happened last night."

"Oh, yeah. Mighty peculiar," Finnerty said.

A short silence, except for the clank and tink of pots and pans inside the wagon, the muffled scrape of tools loosened by the jarring motion of the wagon over rough terrain.

"What do you mean, Fingers?"

"Sometime last night, someone broke into the chuck and stole food."

"What food?"

"Mostly stuff that won't spoil for a time: jerky, hardtack, coffee beans, some salt pork, and bacon, a few peaches in airtights. Well, one or two, I guess. Didn't hear 'em 'cause I was sleepin' some ways away, you know, and the mules was unhitched."

"Who do you figure?" Dag asked.

"Dunno. Could be anybody."

"What about you, Jo? Any ideas?"

She shook her head. "I didn't hear anything either. Whoever stole the chuck went about it awful quiet-like."

"So nobody you can name? Either of you?"

"Coulda been one of the hands or an Injun," Finnerty said. "They took enough grub to last 'em maybe a week or so."

Dag pondered these revelations. Anyone in the outfit wouldn't need to steal grub. He would just have to ask Fingers for a handout and the cook would have been happy to supply whatever was asked.

"Did you pass out grub to Matlee and his bunch?"

"Sure," Finnerty said. "Hardtack and jerked beef. He said they'd be out for a while. He took coffee beans and some other stuff. Said he'd shoot quail or jackrabbits if they ran short of meat. Nobody had to steal nothin' from that outfit."

They were all silent for a while. They reached the rim of the canyon and Finnerty turned the wagon north.

"I'm going to ride up ahead and look for bad dog holes," Dag said. "Just follow me."

"Felix," Jo said, "before you go, I do have one man in mind that might have stolen the food last night. I can't prove it and I may be way wrong."

"Who might that be?" Dag asked.

"Well, I noticed one man in the early evening pay a whole lot of attention to Daddy when he packed up after supper and I put the dishes and utensils away. He kept glancing over as he sat by the fire, smoking a cigarette and belching."

"All right, who was that?"

"Don Horton," she said.

"Horton?"

"Yes, I know that's not much proof of anything, but he was mighty interested in the wagon, all of a sudden like."

"Thanks, Jo. Time will tell," he said, then rode away from the wagon.

Horton again. The man might be up to something. He bore watching. But if he did steal so much food, not wanting anyone to know he took it, what did that mean? What in hell was he planning to do?

Dag wondered if he would ever know. But he had a strong hunch that he would. And maybe he wouldn't have to wait long for Horton to play out his hand and reveal his cards.

Chapter 16

Two more days of driving through the canyon, until they were well past the prairie dog town. Now Flagg was looking for a place to drive the cattle back up on the flat. The water was just trickling through the canyon and the cattle were beginning to grumble. The men had hit patches where the grass was scarce and at night Flagg ordered men to cut off prickly pear, scrape the spines off, and feed them to the weakest cattle at the rear. It wasn't enough, but it kept the herd from running off at every bend where they could smell water.

Up on the flat, Dag could smell the urine and cowpies when the wind was right. At mealtimes, the crew halted by a game trail leading down into the canyon, where the men could walk up and get their grub. At night, Dag, Jo, and Fingers sat by the fire, talking beneath the stars. They'd had no trouble avoiding the prairie dog town, although once or twice, the two men had had to take shovels and fill in holes that the mules might drop a leg into. They managed, though, to stay ahead of the slow-moving herd.

Matlee showed up on the third day, with more than three hundred head of cattle, the hands branded well into the night and the next morning before all were turned into the herd.

"We're gettin' there, Dag," Flagg said.

"Yeah, real slow though."

"We still got a long ways to go before we hit the Red, and they's ranches on both sides of the canyon—and lots of gullies and brush where the wild ones can hide."

"I saw a bunch of my men riding out this morning," Dag said. "Hunting outlaws?"

"Yep. And Matlee's boys are hard at it too. We also picked up a few head in the canyon that just joined up with us. Lonesome, I reckon."

Dag chortled. "Every little bit helps," he said.

"Well, we don't need as many hands and there's plenty of wild cattle in this part of Texas. We'll make do."

"Sure, Jubal."

It wasn't until the next day that Dag had a chance to talk with Matlee. He had come in late the night before, to the chuck wagon and used the cookfire to heat the irons. He and his men branded sixteen head and ran them down into the canyon to join the herd, which was bedded down for the night. There was much lowing and the whinnying of horses as the strange cattle mingled with the growing herd.

"I haven't seen Horton about," Dag said. "He didn't come in with you?"

"Naw, Don said he was going to scout ahead the other day. Haven't seen him since."

"He have grub to do that?"

"He didn't ask for none. So I guess so. How come you want to know about that?"

Dag told him about the chuck wagon break-in some four or five days before.

"Mighty peculiar," Matlee said.

"Yeah, ain't it, though?"

"Are you thinkin' Horton stole that grub?"

"Well, put two and two together, Barry: Horton's gone, and he didn't ask you for no grub.

If he knew he was goin' to be ridin' off by hisself, all he had to do was ask Fingers for some extra chuck."

"I see what you mean, Dag." Matlee lifted his hat and scratched his pate. "Don't make no sense, you put it that way."

"No, it don't. Unless Horton was huntin' somethin' else like."

"Like what?"

"I dunno. Maybe me. When Jo and I went fishin' a few nights ago, somebody took a shot at me or her at that catfish pond."

"First I heard of it."

"Yeah. I haven't told anyone. But Jo said he was watchin' me all the time, and before you and your boys lit out, he was eyein' the chuck wagon, seein' what all Fingers put away and where he put it. You take three or four suspicions like that and you got a whole passel of evidence. Maybe circumstantial, but evidence none the damned less."

"Boy, Dag, you better, by God, be sure before you accuse a good cowhand like Horton of such shenanigans."

"I've been studyin' on that some, Barry, the past few days."

Dag pulled the makings from his pocket and

handed the sack to Matlee. Matlee took the tobacco and Dag fished out the papers and
handed those to him. Barry rolled a cigarette,
licked it tight, and stuck it in his mouth. He
handed the makings back to Dag, who rolled
a quirly for himself. Then he struck a match
and lit Matlee's cigarette and his own.

The two men, deep in thought, pulled a few
puffs from their cigarettes.

"So, Dag, what do you figure?" Matlee
asked.

"I never had no quarrel with Don Horton.
Barely know the man. Flagg said he's worked
many a gather with the hombre and vouches
for him. I ain't seen nothin' to make me feel
different."

"Maybe he's not the jasper who took a shot
at you, Dag."

"Might not be. But as I said, I got to thinkin',
what with all these suspicions rollin' around in
my head, and then I went back to a time just
before we left on this drive."

"And?"

"And Deuce come over to the house and
raised pure Cain 'cause he said I stole Horton
and Manny from him when I didn't know a
damned thing about it. He went and bought

the papers on my spread and threatened to take my land and house if I didn't make my payment next year."

"Deuce is a devil. A hard man in a trade."

"So what if, before Horton left, Deuce offered him some money to rub me out so's I couldn't make that payment?"

Matlee let out a low whistle and shook his head. "Well, Deuce is a mighty hard man and he has the scruples of a dog in heat. I sure wouldn't put something like that past the son of a bitch."

"That's what I thought."

"Well, I reckon you just got to keep your eyes peeled, Dag. And watch your back."

"Yeah," Dag said, feeling an emptiness in the pit of his stomach.

The days passed with no sign of Horton. Flagg told Dagstaff that it was time to run the herd out of the canyon and back on to the plain.

"We're just movin' too slow and there ain't enough grass to fatten the cows no more."

The herd had swelled even more with many of the hands riding out at night and during the day to scout for outlaws. Dag wasn't keeping an exact tally, but he knew they had close to three thousand head, which was encouraging.

" 'Sides," Flagg said, "I been seein' Injun sign."

"You have? Tracks?"

"Tracks. Some old, some more recent like."

"Well, we know there are Comanch' and Kiowa huntin' this canyon, livin' in it."

"Yesterday, I saw what looked like mirror flashes up ahead of us. Could have been the sunshine glancin' off rocks, but I don't think so."

"We got plenty of men, Jubal. They might think twice before comin' at us."

"Stealin' is in a redskin's blood. I doubled the nighthawks when we bedded the herd down, just in case."

"Good idea," Dag said.

The next morning, Flagg found a place where the canyon wall to the west dipped low and the slope wasn't so steep. He ordered the outriders to bunch up the herd while he ran the lead cow up the slope. The herd followed in a steady stream of horns and cowhides, the cows lowing like a bunch of grumbling stockyard beeves going to slaughter.

There were plenty of grass on the plain and creeks running well. Prairie flowers grew as far as a man could see, and the moon rose like an alabaster planet every night, growing full again.

And still Dag saw no sign of Horton. Nor did Flagg see any more signal mirrors flashing in the sun, if that was what he had seen in the first place.

Matlee was scouring the country with his men, bringing in some cattle every time he came back; the branding irons were kept hot, it seemed, all day long and into the night.

At the chuck wagon one evening, when many of the hands from both ranches were finished with supper, sitting around, jawing and smoking, Finnerty spoke to Jimmy.

"You didn't bring your git-tar, Jimmy?" Fingers said.

"Naw, Fingers. Figgered the remuda would take up all my time. And it do."

Finnerty laughed. "I brought one, just in case."

"Just in case what?" Gough asked.

"In case your fingers got to itchin'. Want to play us a tune or two?"

Jimmy smiled. "You read my mind, Bill? My fingers have been plumb lonesome for a set of wire strings."

"This'uns got catgut."

"That'll do."

So Finnerty brought out the worn Mexican guitar. Jimmy tuned it like a master and began to play "Buffalo Gals." Jo stood next to Dag and some of the men began to join in on the chorus. When he livened up the music, some of the men started dancing the jig like drunken fools.

Jo turned to Dag. "Dance with me, Felix?"

"Onliest way I could dance them jigs was if I dropped a lighted cigarette butt down in my pants."

She laughed and took his hands in hers. "I'll show you," she said, and whirled him into the center of the dancing circle of man. The hands started clapping time to the music as the two pranced like an old married couple. Jo was smiling and Dag looked as if he were experiencing a hair-raising ride on a runaway mustang.

Jimmy saw the two dancing, and he played a slow piece the next time around. Dag protested, mildly, when Jo held on to him, but the two looked right graceful there under the light of the moon and glow of the fire. After that, others wanted to dance with Jo and she obliged them, much to Dag's relief. But watching her with the others made him a little green with jealousy, and he wondered again why Jo stirred up such feelings in him.

It might have gone on like that a while longer, but the music stopped with a startling abruptness when they heard gunshots from far out on the plain. Then they heard loud shouts in English, followed by the chilling, high-pitched screeches that sounded too much like war cries.

"Son of a bitch," Flagg said. "Boys, strap on your irons and grab your horses. We got big trouble."

Jo looked at Dag with alarm; her eyes flared and got smoky with fear. Dag got up and went for his horse.

"Felix, be careful," she said.

But he didn't hear her. All he heard was the shrill, tongue-trilling cries of Comanches on the warpath. And when he got to Nero and was putting him under saddle, the horse was as nervous as a long-tailed cat in a room full of rocking chairs.

And Dag's stomach, when he stepped into the saddle, was swarming with flying insects feeling exactly like fear.

Chapter 17

The night filled with the piercing screams of Comanches in full, bloodcurdling cry. Men rode away from the remuda alone, in pairs, and in bunches. Dag rode toward the sounds, his Henry jutting from its scabbard, his .44/40 snug in its holster. Nero kept trying to turn in the opposite direction and Dag had to make him fight the bit with every tug of the reins.

The moon cast a ghostly glow over the herd, their backs painted a dull pewter, their horns glinting pale silver. So far, the herd had not begun to stampede, but cows were bawling in terror and Dag saw that some were jostling one another as if trying to flee. His heart seemed like a lump in his throat as he rode toward the

eerie sound of war songs. So far, he had heard
no more shots, but he dreaded the possibility.
It would not take much now to throw the cattle
herd into a panic and start them running in
every direction.

He could not see much, but he kept riding,
hunching over the saddle horn as if he were
in a race, keeping a low profile, for when the
shooting started, any stray bullet or ball could
find him in the darkness.

Then he saw a commotion up ahead, on the
other side of the herd. Horses raced back and
forth and beyond; a stream of Comanche ponies streaked along in a wide circle as if to
surround the cowhands. It was a fine display
of horsemanship that he could not help but ad-
mire, even though he knew he was watching
a powerful enemy that could kill them all if
their numbers were great enough.

He heard the nighthawks yelling now, hurl-
ing insults at the Comanche.

"Get on outta here."

"Yo, you red bastards."

"You sons of bitches, come on."

Dag knew what the Comanche plan was
now. As he drew closer, he saw that they were
riding just out of range, lifting their bows over

their heads, brandishing their lances, taunting the cowhands to shoot. Well, he thought, the hands were smart enough to figure it out and he wondered who the men were who rode herd that night. He was damned proud of them for holding their fire. And he was a little bit relieved that the Comanches evidently had no pistols or rifles.

Flagg had been smart to double the herders who were on watch. He glanced at the tail end of the herd and saw two riders. That was smart too because the Comanches could very well reverse course and run off some of those cattle while the ones at the head of the herd provided a distraction.

He waved at the riders so that they would not think he was a Comanche, and continued toward the head of the herd, where the Indians were circling. He passed two nighthawks in the dark. He slowed his horse to a walk, then halted for a moment.

"That you, Dag?"

"Yeah, hold your positions."

"Yes, sir. Them Comanch' just started in on us."

"Skip, that you?"

"Yep. Me'n Mendoza got this flank." Skip

Hughes rode for Matlee, but he had worked on the D Slash a few summers ago. He had married Matlee's sister, Lynne Ann, and that was why he had left to work for his brother-in-law. In summer, he wrote poetry and both he and his wife taught school—arithmetic, Dag thought. He didn't know what Lynne Ann taught, but he thought it had to do with reading.

"Hold your fire unless they get right on top of you, Skip. You too, Ricardo."

"Will do, Dag," Skip replied and Ricardo Mendoza grunted an assent in Spanish.

Dag rode on, staring at the Comanches rounding the cattle at the head of the herd. By now the bawling was loud and the cattle even more restless. He listened for a change in pitch that would tell him they had found a leader who would run so that they could follow. Cattle were herd animals and they followed the strongest cow or, in case of a stampede, they followed the most scared, which was often the cow just in front of them.

"Spread out, spread out," Flagg was saying. "Stay low and don't shoot unless you can smell Injun breath."

The Comanches kept riding back and forth, teams of them going in opposite directions. It was confusing to Dag at first, but then the Comanches changed their tactics. While one bunch was going one way, another would ride in close, as if to cut a few heads out of the herd. Then these would dart back out and another group would flash in, yelling and yipping like a pack of wild dogs.

Dag drew his pistol and backed Nero into the herd, which was milling around, bawling and snorting. He could see the fear in their roiling wide eyes as they backed away. But the horses and riders seemed to give them some comfort, as if they knew they were being protected.

All of a sudden, the war cries died out and the Comanches changed their tactics again, riding their ponies straight at the herd so that they were within rifle range. They thrust with their horses, trying to rattle the cowhands guarding the herd. They would gallop in, turn their horses on a ten-cent piece, then dash back out. Back and forth, in small groups, the Comanches taunted the white men, calling out insults in their native tongue, screaming, yelling as they drew close, only to turn their horses with their knees at the last minute, riding off, their bodies hugging the bare backs of their ponies.

"Don't shoot," Flagg said. "Pass the word."

Dag heard the men pass the warning all along the herd, where nervous nighthawks with itchy fingers waited, ready to shoot, wanting to shoot, but dreading a stampede almost more than they feared the Indians.

"They sure as hell can't keep this up all night," Dag said.

"The hell they can't," Flagg said.

But the Comanches, after riding clear around the herd, as if looking for a weak spot so that they could run off a few head of cattle, finally drifted away into the darkness. It got so quiet, Dag felt as if he were in a huge room with all the air sucked out of it. A vacuum. Then the nighthawks started crooning to the cattle, riding slow to calm them down. After a while, the lowing and caterwauling died down and the herd started bedding down again.

"Whew," Dag said.

" 'Whew' is right," Flagg said. "We almost had a real big mess here."

"Think they're gone for good, Jubal?"

"Hell, that was just their way of testing us. I reckon they'll come up with another idea, right soon."

"What do they want? Some cattle to eat?"

"No, I reckon it's more than that. These were

warriors. They want blood. We're on what they reckon is their land and they're going to give us hell as long as we're here."

"They didn't have guns, anyway," Dag said, holstering his pistol.

"Nope, but they probably want ours." Flagg turned away and started issuing orders. "Those of you who ain't tendin' herd, get on back to the chuck wagon one at a time and don't make no noise. We'll keep a double guard, same shifts."

Dag just then thought of the chuck wagon. Fingers and Jo were there, along with Jimmy and Little Jake—not much of a force if the Comanches wanted to attack and steal food. But they had ridden off to the north, in the opposite direction. Of course, he knew they could circle around. He sighed and rode gingerly past the cows around him, then turned back toward camp. He was worried.

Who are you worried about? he asked himself, silently. But he already knew the answer. *Jo.* He hated to think what a band of savages like the Comanches would do to her if they ever captured her alive. He shuddered. These were not good thoughts, he knew, and he tried to drive them out of his mind.

Jo walked out to meet Dag when he returned. "What happened?" she asked.

"The Comanches run off, Jo."

"I didn't hear any more shots."

"Thank God. That herd would have scattered like leaves in autumn. We'd be days trackin' 'em all down."

"I was worried about you, Felix."

"No need."

"Still I worry about you."

He swung out of the saddle. "Jo, don't," he said.

But she wasn't listening, evidently. She came up to him and put a hand on his arm. "Felix, you know I care about you, don't you?"

"I reckon."

"Don't you care about me?"

Dag started to squirm inside his skin. "I care about you plenty, Jo, but not that way."

"What way?"

"You know," he said.

"No, I don't know."

"Well, I can't rightly explain it, Jo. I got to unsaddle Nero, hobble him up for the night."

"Don't keep running away, Felix."

"I ain't runnin' from nothin', Jo."

She laughed. "Like a rabbit," she said. "I'll help you unsaddle Nero."

"Jo, I don't need no help." He paused, softening. "But you can tag along if you like."

"I like," she said and squeezed his arm with her hand.

They walked back from the remuda together. Dag's thoughts raced. He felt all mixed up. Truth was, he liked Jo's company. And he admitted to himself that he was flattered by her interest in him and her attentions. She did special little things when she thought no one was paying much attention, a touch on his back or his shoulder at chow, giving him an extra spoonful of blackberry jelly or honey for his biscuits. Brief smiles and sometimes, a wink.

Now, in the darkness, he looked at her. Her mouth was like a small rose in the firelight when they got back to camp.

"You want some coffee, Felix?" she asked.

"Naw, my heart's pumpin' fast as it is."

"Because of the Comanches?" she said. "Or do I do that to you?"

"Jo, you are a bold woman—that's for danged sure."

"You think so, Felix? Heck, I haven't even shown you my bold side." She laughed, but what she said tugged at his heart.

"Spare me," he joked.

She took his arm in hers, squeezed him close to her. Fingers was sitting by the fire, smoking a last pipe before turning in. Cowhands were sprawled in a wide circle some distance from the chuck wagon, rifles at their sides, pistols close at hand. One man was snoring.

"I might take pity on you, Felix, and spare you my embarrassing boldness. I might." She squeezed his arm again and he felt a thrilling ripple of pleasure course through him like a velvety shot of electricity.

"I'm going to turn in, Jo. Uh, thanks for walkin' with me—ah, coming out with me, I mean."

"I know what you mean," she said and turned to face him, releasing her hold on his arm. Then she put her hands on his shoulders and stood on tiptoe. She pecked him on the lips with that red bud of a mouth of hers, then danced away.

"Good night," she said. "Sleep tight. Pleasant dreams."

Dag stood there, speechless, his lips burning as if they had been brushed lightly with stinging nettles—or touched by a sudden, searing fire that was beyond understanding and like nothing he had ever felt before.

Chapter 18

Flagg rode well ahead of the herd, scouting the best terrain, the best grass, and the fewest chances of ambush by marauding Indians. Dag rode beside him, both of them setting the pace for the chuck wagon, which had been taking the lead for several weeks. Flagg had kept it in the rear for some days because of the way the herd acted after leaving the home range. Cattle fought to return for at least three days, and this herd, because it had grown so much, had been especially hard to handle. Now it had to follow the pace of the chuck wagon so that they wouldn't lose time when it came to the drovers and mealtimes. The noon meal was served when the sun was straight up, and supper at sundown. Period.

Over the past weeks, Flagg had slowed the drive down considerably so that they could trail brand the cattle they now had, which numbered close to thirty-three hundred head. The trail brands were used to identify the herd in case it got mixed in with another. Flagg had chosen the brand, which was placed on the right hip of their cattle. It was the QC, which stood for Quitaque-Cheyenne.

"Somebody's coming," Dag said, pointing ahead. "Can't make out who it is, friend or foe."

Flagg looked at the two specks on the horizon. They were riding over a vast island of grass and the herd was fattening up, moving slow, behind them.

"Friend, I'd say," Flagg said. "They ain't movin' fast and they're headed straight for us."

"Tall horses," Dag said. "Not ponies."

"You're gettin' good at this, Felix," Flagg said. "Them weeks ridin' swing and flank and drag didn't do you no harm."

Dag laughed. "I rode point too."

"Yeah, you did."

The point riders were on either side of the herd at the front. They saw to it that the lead steer, which had replaced the cow that started out in that position, stayed on course and kept moving. About a third of the way behind them rode the swing riders, and back another third were the flank riders. The drag riders brought up the rear of the herd and were responsible for turning any cattle that tried to go back to the home range or anywhere else they weren't supposed to go.

Dagstaff and Flagg kept riding toward the two approaching riders. When the two strangers got close, Dag saw that they were cowmen. The lariats hanging from their saddles looked well worn, and they had that look about them: dusty, battered hats, wind- and sun-weathered faces, and dirt-caked lines around their mouths.

"Howdy," one of the men said, the taller of the two. "I'm Paul Gustafsen, and this is my segundo, Dave Franklin. We're from the Double C spread, just a stone's chunk from here. Folks call me Gus."

"I'm Jubal Flagg, the trail boss, and this is the rancher who hired me, Felix Dagstaff. We call him Dag, among other things."

Gus laughed. "I saw your dust," he said,

"wondered if you boys would like to drive some of my herd to the railhead. You headed for Abilene?"

"No," Dag said, "farther west and north. Better money."

"Smoke?" Dave said, pulling the makings from his pocket.

"Sure," Dag said, extending his hand out for the sack of tobacco.

"I'll cut me a chaw," Flagg said, digging out a twist from his shirt pocket.

Dag rolled a cigarette, wet it down with his spit, and handed the sack back to Gus, who rolled one and handed the sack to Franklin. Dag lit their cigarettes, then his, while Flagg stuffed a cut-off chunk of tobacco into his mouth, folded up his Barlow pocketknife, and put it away.

"Good market for beef where you're goin'?" Gus asked, a casual tone to his voice.

"Fair to middlin'," Dag said.

"Are you full up, or could you drive some of my herd up to wherever you're goin'?"

"How many head?" Flagg asked. He was still the trail boss, and this concerned him as much as it did Dag.

"Oh, maybe seven hunnert or so. I been waitin' for a drive to come this way. You're the first I've seen all spring."

"What kind of price are you lookin' for?" Dag asked, not wanting to appear too eager. Gus, though, just might be the answer to his prayers. Outlaw cattle were scarce in these parts.

"Oh, I'd be right satisfied with anything over fifteen dollars a head," Gus said.

Dag's eyebrows arched. He couldn't help it. Maybe dreams did come true. He looked at Flagg, who nodded almost imperceptibly.

"We could maybe do a mite better than that, Gus," Dag said. "How many hands can you put with us?"

"Only a couple. That be enough?"

"We have plenty of drovers," Flagg said. "Two men would work just fine, I reckon."

Gus smiled. So did Dave.

"We could maybe put twenty or twenty-five greenbacks in your hand for each head that finished the drive," Dag said. "That do?"

"That would be just fine—uh, Dag, is it?"

"Yes."

"Wish I could go with you. But we've had Comanche trouble round here lately. That's one reason I want to thin my herd."

The three men with quirlys smoked. Flagg chewed and spat.

"You got water on your spread for my herd?" Flagg asked. "We could maybe bed down there tonight and trail brand your seven hunnert head."

"I got a big lake and the spring rains have kept the water high, up to the brim."

"Let's shake on it," Dag said. He and Gus shook hands.

"We'll ride along with you," Gus said, "show you my lake. How many head you driving?"

Dag told him. Gus whistled in surprise.

"Boy," he said, "that's a goodly number, all right."

"Mex cattle," Flagg said. "They fatten up on the hoof."

"So you're not going to the railhead in Kansas," Gus said.

"Cheyenne," Dag said. "We'll get a better price up yonder. Guaranteed."

"That's good enough for me."

They passed the chuck wagon and all waved at Fingers and Jo as they passed. Dag saw a questioning look on Jo's face, but he only smiled. It would be something to talk about that night, he mused. Another good excuse to spend time with her, while he mentally kicked himself for his disloyalty to Laura and his infatuation with Jo Finnerty.

The ride took an hour and a half before they were on Double C land. Gus made a slight turn over gently rolling land. A pair of mourning doves knifed through the sky on whistling wings, and quail piped somewhere out of sight. They topped a rise and Dag's eyes widened at what he saw.

There, before them, stood a large lake, perhaps ten or fifteen acres in size, and beyond, and surrounding it, a fine carpeting of grass that looked to be bluestem mixed in with other types that he couldn't identify.

"You've got quite a spread here, Gus," Dag said. "Where'd you get that seed?"

"Some imported from Kentucky, some from England, some from Africa. I'm thinkin' about mix-breeding my cattle too, maybe gettin' some British breeds in here, Herefords and such. I heard you could cross-breed 'em with longhorns and get cattle with a larger frame, more beef on the hoof."

"I wish you good luck," Dag said.

"You might want to think about it yourself, down the road."

"I will."

"Let's ride on up to the cattle I'd like you to drive for me and I'll introduce you to the drovers I'll send along with you."

They rode around the lake, through more fields where cattle ranged. Gus had done a lot of land clearing, yet it seemed all groomed. He had left brush and trees for game cover, and each pasture had at least one tank, large watering holes. The cattle Dagstaff and Flagg saw all looked healthy and fat.

The ranch house was surrounded by out buildings. There were a stable, a barn, several corrals, horses grazing in a nearby pasture, a bunkhouse, and a smokehouse. The house itself was a frame dwelling that had been added to over the years with what looked to Dag like whipsawed lumber. There were even froed shingles on the roof, which surprised him. Someone had gone to a lot of trouble to build such a place.

The men tied up their horses to a hitchrail in front of the house.

"Come on in," Gus said.

Dag looked at Flagg. They were both filthy, their clothes soaked with grease and caked with dust, their boots smelling of cowshit and horse dung.

"Ah," Dag said, "maybe Jubal and I should just sit out on your porch. We ain't had a proper bath in some time and we got our trail duds on."

"Suit yourself," Gus said. "I'll have the missus bring us some hot coffee, or we got tea. No ice though, but she keeps it in an *olla* in the shade, so it stays right cool."

"Maybe tea," Flagg said, the wrinkle of a smile on his lips. "We ain't had no tea in many a moon."

"Yeah, tea," Dag said, his mouth starting to water. It would be a change from Fingers' coffee, which was thick enough to float nails in.

There was a swing on the porch and several chairs. Dave sat down and took off his hat. He waved Dag and Jubal to chairs.

"Feels good to get out of the heat," Dave said. "You boys come a long ways?"

Flagg sat down, then got up again, walked to the porch railing, and spat out a chewed wad of tobacco. He wiped his mouth with his sleeve and rubbed his brown teeth.

"Yeah, it's been a ride," Dag said.

"Any trouble?"

"Comanches one night."

"Anybody hurt?"

"Naw, they run off. They had only bows and arrows, lances. Testing us, I think."

"Well, them savages is mighty patient sometimes. We run 'em off here all the time. Kiowas too. Sometimes Apaches. From here to the Red you better keep your eyes peeled."

"Thanks for the advice," Dag said, as Flagg sat down.

Gus came back out onto the porch and sat down in a chair.

"The missus will be right out with the tea. She gets it from a mercantile up in Amarillo."

"We must be getting close to that town," Dag said.

"Another two to three weeks driving, maybe," Gus said. "Our boys make it in three or four days."

A woman came out of the house carrying a tray with a sugar bowl and spoon and four jelly glasses gleaming amber in the sun. She handed a glass to each of the men.

"I'm Janet," she said. "But, everybody calls me Jan. There's sugar here if you've got a sweet tooth." She was a petite, dark-haired woman with a warm smile.

"Thanks, Jan," Gus said. "Just set the tray on that little table there."

Janet left the tray and went back into the house.

"Tastes good," Dag said, after taking a sip of tea.

Flagg was spooning sugar into his. "Say, how'd you know we were headed this way?" Flagg asked. "Been curious about that. Did your hands spot our chuck wagon?"

"As a matter of fact, no," Gus said. "Feller come through here, oh a week ago, I reckon, and said they was a big herd comin' up our way."

Flagg sat up straight. "Did the feller have a name?" he asked.

"Said his name was Horton. Don Horton, wasn't it, Dave?"

"Yep, that's the name."

Dag shot a look at Jubal, his eyes glittering with alarm. He had almost forgotten about Horton in the past few weeks. He wondered what the man was up to, and why he had told Gus about the herd. Suddenly, all his feelings about the man boiled up in his mind and he knew that, sooner or later, Horton would show up again. A lot closer, maybe, the next time.

Chapter 19

There was a long moment of silence on the porch, as if time had suddenly stopped dead still.

"You know the man?" Gus asked.

Flagg recovered more quickly than Dag. "He's one of our drovers," Flagg said, "off scouting."

"Well, he gave me the idea to ask you to drive my cattle up north with you. The money will allow me to buy some English stock for cross-breeding."

"I'd better get back to the herd," Flagg said, finishing off his tea and standing up. "Please tell the missus how much I liked her tea on a hot afternoon."

A slight breeze stirred the two hanging plants that were suspended from the ceiling on small chains. They exuded the faint aroma of lilacs.

Flagg shook hands with Gus and Dave. "You can stay here if you like, Dag."

"I'll go with you, Jubal. I think we're finished here." He turned to Gus. "Have your herd ready when we pass through, Gus. I'll take care of the rest. Handshake?"

"Sure, Felix."

The two men shook hands.

"All of your stock branded?" Flagg asked.

"Yep, ever' head."

"We'll trail brand 'em before we turn 'em into the herd."

"My hands can help with that."

"No need."

"When we come out, I'll bring the two hands I'm sending with the herd. You'll meet 'em then."

Felix and Jubal rode off, heading back the way they had come. Neither spoke until they were well away from ranch headquarters. They saw riders, who waved at them. They waved back. Doves coursed the sky, in pairs, darting past in swift undulating wing strokes, whistling softly.

"All right, Jubal," Dag said, "what do you make of Horton bein' up here at the Double C?"

"It don't make a whole lot of sense, I reckon."

"He ever been up this way before?" Dag asked.

"Why, he grew up around Amarillo. I think his pa had a spread on the salt fork of the Red, matter of fact."

"So he knows the country."

"Pretty much."

Dag mulled over in his mind what he knew, what he suspected. He was pretty sure that Horton had tried to kill him once. And then he had left suddenly. Now his track had shown up here. He was heading north, toward the Red River. Why? Was he waiting somewhere up ahead in ambush? At some place where he had the advantage of concealment and surprise? How did a man protect himself against a drygulcher like that?

As they rode, Dag's scalp prickled and he began to look around as if expecting to see Horton materialize over the horizon at any moment. He wondered why Horton wanted to kill him. But it didn't take a big stretch of the imagination to see who would benefit from his death: Deutsch.

Flagg broke into Dag's reverie. "Did you know, Dag, that most trail bosses don't let the drovers bring their own horses to the remuda, like we did?"

"No, I didn't know that."

"Yep. It's kind of like a guarantee, you know?"

"A guarantee? Of what?"

"Well, not only that we have good horses suited for such purposes, but if a drover deserts the herd, as some do, then he's guilty of a crime. He's a thief."

"Hm. I never knew that," Dag said.

"You know. Cowhands get to a town after being months on the trail and some of 'em get real drunk and raise hell. Sometimes a man will meet a gal that he thinks is the most beautiful and saintly female on earth. Most often she's some whore he met in a saloon, and in the dark, with all that paint, she looks like Cleopatra. So he'll stay behind, sell the horse he's on, and get married. If he survives that, when the trail boss and the other drovers come back through the town, they find the deserter and hang him for a damned horsethief."

"What's the point, Dag? Horton brought his own horse."

"Yeah, he did. He rode his own horse, but if you noticed, whenever he went out lookin' for outlaws, he always took one of the horses in Jimmy's remuda."

"I didn't notice, no."

"Well, when he lit a shuck from the herd, he wasn't straddlin' his own horse."

"What're you drivin' at, Jubal?"

"I'm sayin', if we run into Don up ahead somewheres, and he's on that horse, I'm going to drag his ass from it and hang him from the nearest goddamned tree."

"You'd hang him?"

"Faster'n you can say 'Johnny Jumpup.'"

Dag rubbed his neck and squinted up at the blue sky, up toward where he imagined heaven to be. He looked at Jubal, whose expression hadn't changed. He had no doubt that Jubal was a man of his word. If they ran into Horton, he knew Jubal would show him no mercy. To him, a horsethief was a horsethief.

"I think Horton tried to kill me one night, Jubal."

"What?"

Dag told him about the incident at the pond and what Jo had told him.

"Why in hell didn't you tell me, Dag?"

"I couldn't prove it."

"Well, that says a lot about why he left. And you think Deuce might be behind it? Offered Don some cash money to put out your lamp?"

"I wouldn't put it past Deuce."

A few seconds flowed by like water in a creek.

"Neither would I," Flagg said.

They stopped at the chuck wagon, where Flagg told Fingers where to go and set up for supper. Jo got down and walked over to talk to Dag.

"Well," she said, "you've got your herd, Felix. That must make you pretty happy."

"If it holds up, we've got enough cattle to fill my contract."

"I pray it does," she said.

"Horton was up here first. Gus, the rancher of the Double C, told us he was by a couple of weeks ago."

Her expression froze on her face. A worried look crept into her eyes like fumes from a smoldering fire.

"Felix, be careful. He might be up ahead waiting to . . ." She couldn't finish her thought.

"I know," he said. "Don't worry. He's not

going to catch me with my pants down. Uh, I mean—"

She laughed. "I know what you mean. Just you be right careful, hear?"

"I will," he said.

She put a hand on Dag's leg. The pressure made his skin feel as if he had been touched by a branding iron.

By late afternoon, the herd came up to the lake and Flagg let the cattle go to drink. The drovers fanned out and watches were set for the evening. Those not on first watch unsaddled their horses and gathered around the chuck wagon, where Jubal issued further orders.

"The head honcho's going to bring us seven hunnert more head to drive to Cheyenne," he said. "I want you, Lonnie, to pick some hands to help you heat up the irons and trail brand ever' head before we move out tomorrow."

There was much grumbling among the men, but Cavins took over, drew the QC irons from the wagon, and instructed them to make four separate fires out in the open, well away from the lake and the chuck wagon.

As soon as the herd was settled down, Flagg rode off toward the Double C ranch house.

About an hour later, Gus's men began driving small bunches of cattle to each branding fire.

Flagg, along with Gus and Dave, rode up to find Dag, with two other men.

"Dag, these are the drovers from the Double C who'll continue the drive with us."

"This here's Tom Leeds," Gus said, pointing to one of the men, a short, stocky man with a taciturn expression on his ruddy face. He had a bedroll and a sougan behind his saddle, as did the other drover. "And this other'n is Vince Sutphen. Both good men, hard workers, with the usual cowboy vices."

Dag laughed and shook hands with both men. "Welcome," he said. "You go on over to the chuck wagon and have supper with us, Tom and Vince, and make yourself acquainted with the rest of the hands. Mighty nice to have you along."

"Thank you, Dag," Tom said.

"You got a fine-lookin' bunch of cattle there," Sutphen said. "A pleasure to meet you, Dag."

The two men rode off and Gus heaved a sigh. "They'll do to ride the river with," he said.

"They look like good hands," Flagg said.

"They do," Dag said. "Thank you, Gus. Will

you take supper with us? I think Jo, the cookie's daughter, made cherry pies today."

"No, the missus has a big meal for me, and if I don't get right back, it'll be on the table already and the dogs will eat it."

The men laughed.

"I have a head count of seven hunnert and thirty-five head, most of 'em young beeves and all fit to make the drive," Gus said.

"I'll take your word for it," Flagg said, "but I'll tally 'em and give the sheet to Tom or Vince, whichever you say."

"It don't make me no nevermind," Gus said. "Either one has my trust."

"Then they have ours too," Flagg said.

Flagg said goodbye to Gus and Dave and then slipped out of the saddle.

"I'll walk back with you, Dag. I feel pretty good about this. It looks like we made our quota. Thanks, maybe, to Don Horton."

"Yeah, that's so. Maybe the man's heart ain't all black."

"I'm mighty curious about that jasper, though. He's done run way off the track and I'll be damned if I know why."

"Maybe, after he kills me, he'll want to come back to the drive," Dag said, "figures a favor like this won't do him no harm. You couldn't rightly hang a man for doing us a good turn, could you, Jubal?"

"I'd as soon hang him for murder as for stealin' a horse. But we're not going to let him kill you, Dag. Starting tomorrow, I'm going to tell every rider what we think he's done or is goin' to do, and I'm gonna put a bounty on Horton's head with my own cash money."

"You don't have to do that, Jubal. I can take care of myself."

"I know you can, Dag. But the more eyes we have out there, the better the chance one of us will spot him before he can drygulch you."

"That gives me some small comfort, Jubal."

But it didn't. That was the beginning of constant worry for Felix Dagstaff. Little did he know he would have other worries nearly as large before the drive ended in Cheyenne.

He would take Horton's dark mission to bed every night and wake up with the worry on his shoulders every morning. It would be like lugging an oxen yoke that weighed a hundred pounds and was made, not of wood, but of iron.

Chapter 20

When Flagg woke up the next morning, he expected to see Manny Chavez shaking him out of his bedroll. Instead, it was Dag, hunkered down next to him, already dressed, two cups of steaming coffee in his hands.

"What the hell, Dag? Have you gone plumb loco?"

Dag chuckled. "I'm goin' out with you, Jubal. Now drink this and get into your duds. I want you bright-eyed and bushy-tailed when we ride out. I've got a lot to tell you."

"Oh, yeah? Somethin' I don't know? I don't like surprises, Dag."

"You'll like this one," Dag said, and rose to his feet. As he did so, Flagg sat up and snatched one of the cups out of his hand. He looked like a wraith standing there in his long johns, a blanket draped over his shoulders like a highwayman's cape. He sucked down coffee hot enough to burn an ordinary man's lips.

"I see you got old Nero under saddle already, Dag. You must have a hell of a big burr under your blanket."

Dag sipped his coffee and looked out over the plain. A thin layer of fog hovered just above the lake and seeped out over the cattle herd like a shroud. Off in the trees, Dag saw a small pinpoint of orange light. A cigarette glow? In the predawn darkness it was hard to tell. Perhaps one of the hands had heeded the call to nature and was smoking a quirly in privacy before walking back to his bedroll. The light moved, then vanished; he wondered if he had seen it at all.

"You want to jaw all morning, Jubal? We got trails to ride, rivers to cross."

"Let's skip the fat chewin', Dag, till I've got my eyes full open."

"Trust me, Jubal."

Flagg snorted. "I'll tell Manny to start the herd up after breakfast, when the dew's burned off. The men are tired as hell. They was branding those Double Cs all night, or most of it."

"I know. I never heard so much cow bawling as I did last night. It's a damned wonder our herd didn't stampede to hell and gone."

"I got this herd trained like a bunch of sheep," Flagg said.

"Don't you be usin' that word, Jubal, or I'll have to wash your mouth out with lye soap."

Flagg didn't laugh. He just grunted.

It was chilly, and there was heavy dew on the ground. Flagg drank his coffee, skinned out of his long johns and pulled on his pants and shirt while standing on his ground blanket, wriggling his toes.

He saddled his horse and the two rode away from camp into the darkness, fixing on the North Star for guidance. The black shapes of nighthawks loomed up and Flagg spoke to them before they could challenge them.

"Up early, boss," Fred Reilly, a Box M rider whispered, as they passed.

"I got the eyes of an owl," Flagg said.

A few moments later, out beyond the lake and riding through a stand of hardwoods, live oaks, hickory, and a few mesquite, Dag spoke.

"Who the hell was that, Jubal?"

"Fred Reilly."

"Christ, I ain't been able to recognize even my own hands of late."

"Well, I have a hard time recognizing you, Dag. We're all a bunch of fuzzy faces."

They both touched their beards. None of the men had shaved in weeks. Fingers was about the only one who had scraped hair off his face lately. A few had sneaked over to the creeks they crossed with straight razors, but they were the exception, the younger men.

The moon still rode the sky, thirty degrees above the western horizon, but the sky was paling and many of the stars were winking out like wind-snuffed candles.

They had left the region of Palo Duro Canyon some days before and had been drifting west. In the distance, they heard the yapping of coyotes, a running trill of notes that rippled up and down the treble scale in disembodied song. In the trees, a whip-poor-will croaked its monotonous cry, which sounded like someone stropping leather, and a screech owl answered, sounding like the ghost of one of those nightjars.

A half hour later, they rounded a small ravine and there, stretching into the distance, was an ancient buffalo trail, streaming north-west. Dag reined in and pointed to the vast, uneven plain beyond the buffalo trail.

"That's the cutoff I followed when I rode through here last year, Jubal. If you turn the herd here, we go to the YA, Charlie Good-night's spread. When I stopped in to see him, he showed me a way that will cut twenty days off our drive to Cheyenne."

"I never would have thunk it," Flagg said. "And you rode that way?"

"Sure did, and came back that way too. So it's all fixed in my mind. Jubal, we don't have to cross the Red going this way."

"I was worried about that. We could have lost some cattle crossing the Red, maybe some men too. You're a smart one, Dag. I would have thought we'd go straight north to Kansas and Nebraska and cut over on the South Platte or somewheres."

"Long way around. We head northeast and I have a map all drawn out for you. We even pass through several towns, where we can re-supply and let the men have a little fun and maybe get a shave and a haircut so's we don't ride into Cheyenne lookin' like a bunch of griz-zled prospectors."

Flagg laughed and stroked his beard. It had stopped itching and was beginning to feel like part of his face.

"When do I get the map?" he asked.

"Whenever you want. It's drawn on oilskin and is in my saddlebags now."

"I'll get it tonight then and study it. I like the part about the towns. There's been a lot of grumbling about that, but I didn't want to lose any men in Texas. So I took the drive well away from any clapboards. Civilization spoils a man, sometimes."

By the time Flagg and Dagstaff returned, Manny Chavez had the herd moving. They passed Fingers, Jo, and the chuck wagon on the way back. Flagg gave Fingers directions, told him where to turn west.

"We'll see you at noon," Flagg said.

"Yes, sir, boss," Fingers said, grinning like a Cheshire cat on hard cider.

"I'm excited," Jo said. "New lands, adventure, leaving Texas."

"Let's not hope for too much adventure," Dag said. "But I guarantee you're gonna find the trail interesting."

"See you at noon, Felix," she said, a warmth

in her voice that wrapped around him and seeped into his senses like fragrant silk.

They met at noon at the head of the canyon, with the herd still moving, grazing slowly as they moved northwest. Riders came and went from getting their chuck and riding herd. The hands all looked haggard from working well into the night with the trail branding, but the change in direction seemed to perk them up. The sky began to fill with clouds by late afternoon, huge white galleons sailing in from the west, their sails unfurled in fluffy, bulging billows of cotton, brilliant against a blue sky.

The country was beginning to become more rugged and the cattle had to fan out in a wide area to forage for grass. By that evening, cattle, horses, and men were near exhaustion. Flagg made a decision that they would lie up for most of the following day so that everyone could get some rest before continuing the drive. The new cattle from the Double C were still inclined to turn back toward their home ranch and it was an all-day fight to keep driving them back into the herd.

"A day off will make the Double C cows more tolerant of being driven off their home range," Flagg told everyone. "So rest up and then be prepared for some rugged going."

Dag slept fitfully that night and was glad he didn't have to get up early. But he was in for a rude surprise when, shortly after dawn, he felt himself being shaken out of a sleep that had finally come only an hour or so before.

"What? Who the hell . . . ?"

"Dag, get up," Jimmy Gough said. "I got some bad news."

"Huh?"

"Damn it, Dag. I'm real sorry. I don't know how it happened."

Dag wrestled his blanket from him and sat up, rubbing his hands through his hair and blinking his eyes. For a few seconds he couldn't remember where he was, but then he heard cattle lowing and knew he sure as hell wasn't back in his own house and bed.

"What you got in your craw, Jimmy?"

"Somebody sneaked in a while ago and stole your horse, Dag."

Dag came fully awake. He stood up and looked at Gough as if he had lost his senses.

"Nero?"

"Yeah. I heard some whickering over in the remuda a few minutes ago. I got up and went over there. I saw some tracks and got curious, so I did a head count. It wasn't no Injun, for sure. Somebody wearin' boots come up and stole Nero. He was the onliest horse what was took."

"Damn it, Jimmy. What do you mean it wasn't an Injun?"

"Tracks are plain, Dag. The man was afoot and he wore boots."

Dag dressed quickly and strapped on his six-gun. "Maybe you're mistaken, Jimmy. Let's take a look. Show me them tracks."

The two walked to the remuda, where all the horses were hobbled and grazing on the sparse grasses. Jimmy led him to a bare spot where there were two sets of tracks. Dag recognized Nero's hoofprints. And the man's tracks were definitely not Indian: bootheels gouged into the ground, a clear outline of the soles. The tracks led away from camp, to the north.

"Can you read tracks, Dag?" Jimmy asked.

"I can sure as hell read these. We got us a horsethief, Jimmy."

"But who? There ain't no ranch within miles of here from the look of the land."

"Well, I'm damned sure goin' to find out. Let me pick out a good horse and saddle up. I'll find the bastard."

"In this country, you need a horse with good legs and bottom. How about that little sorrel gelding, Firefly? You rode him before."

"Yeah. I'll saddle up Firefly, get some grub, and light out."

"You ain't plannin' on trackin' by yourself?"

"It's only one man's tracks I see here, Jimmy."

"Yeah, but . . ."

"But what?"

"Could be a whole passel of outlaws where he's a-goin'."

"I'll think about it."

By that time, Flagg and some others were up. Fingers had the breakfast fire going and coffee boiling. Dag had given Flagg the oilskin map the night before and he knew Jubal had stayed late by the fire, studying it.

He told Flagg what had happened and that he was going to track the horsethief.

"You better take somebody with you, Dag. Somebody who's as good a shot as you are."

"Why?"

"You know who you're goin' after, don't you?"

"No, I wish I did."

The two walked over to the remuda so that

Flagg could study the tracks. "I recognize those boots," Flagg said. "You're going to be trackin' a skunk."

"That ain't no news. Any horsethief's a skunk."

"Yeah, Dag, but this one goes by the name of Don Horton."

Dag let the news sink in. Why hadn't he come to that same conclusion? Horton, of course.

"Yeah, Jubal. He stole Nero for a reason, didn't he?"

"He sure as hell did. He don't want the horse, Dag. He wants you."

Dag felt as if someone had slammed him in the gut with a sixteen-pound sledgehammer.

Chapter 21

Dag wanted to know how Flagg recognized the bootprint as Horton's.

"He cut the sole on a boot scraper," Flagg said, "nicked the sole, just before we left Deuce's."

"I saw the nick," Dag said, as he finished saddling Firefly.

"I ought to be going with you, Dag. Could be dangerous."

"I'd rather you stay with the herd, Jubal. I'm taking Lonnie with me."

Even as he said it, Lonnie Cavins rode up on a sorrel gelding, Socks, fifteen hands high with four white stockings and a blaze face—a strong young, horse, with a sound chest. Lonnie had a Sharps carbine jutting from its scabbard and wore a Colt six-shooter in .45 caliber. Another pistol dripped from the saddle horn, a matched Colt. He looked, Dag thought, with his beard and unruly hair clumping from under his hat, like a dirty pipe cleaner all covered with soot. He was as lean and as homely as a dried string bean, but the man was quietly fearless and could use each and every weapon he had close at hand. His pale blue eyes betrayed no emotion.

"Good choice," Flagg said. "Cavins can shoot with the best."

"They called him 'Dead Eye' in the war," Dag said.

"You boys better take some grub with you, and make sure your canteens are filled. Oh, here comes Jo now."

Jo came over with two paper packages. She handed one to Cavins, one to Dag.

"Some hardtack and jerky," she said. "Felix, be careful, won't you?"

In that mysterious grapevine that seemed to have no source or conveyance known to mortal man, half the camp knew about the stolen horse and who the thief was. Men walked up to wish them luck. Their faces blurred as Dag

acknowledged them, impatient to start tracking
Horton. Tracks aged, he knew, and it could
rain and the wind could come up and wipe
out all trace of Nero and Horton.

"We're going, Jubal. Thanks, Jo. I'll be
seeing you."

"Goodbye, Felix," she said, her voice choking up on her so that she had to bite her lip
and turn her head.

Dag turned his horse and he and Cavins
rode out, following the clear tracks on the
ground as if they were markers on a map. For
some reason, he did not wave goodbye.

"*Vaya con Dios*," Flagg said, as he watched
the two ride out on the hunt for Horton.

The tracks led them over hard ground, but
were easy to follow. Dag kept looking ahead
and on both sides of the game trail Horton had
taken. The landscape was bleak, rocky, strewn
with several varieties of cactus and islands of
grass.

"At least we got the sun at our backs," Cavins said.

Dag turned to him and put a finger to his
lips to indicate silence. Cavins nodded, and
they continued for another half hour or so. The
land started to rise, and the only sound was

the ring and clank of their horses' iron shoes on stone.

Then, as they were starting up the shallow slope, Cavins reached over and touched Dag's shoulder. He pointed straight ahead to the top of the knoll.

Dag swallowed hard. There, lit by the sun, his black hide glistening with shots of brilliant light, stood Nero, standing hip shot, gazing down at them, his ears stiff and twitching, his tail flicking at flies.

A rifle shot shattered the silence like the crack of a bullwhip. The sound reverberated in every direction and hung in the air with ominous echoes. Dag felt as if someone had driven a dagger into his heart as he saw Nero go down. The horse kicked its legs for several seconds, then stiffened and lay still.

Dag swore under his breath.

Cavins jerked his carbine from its boot and hunched down in the saddle.

It took Dag a moment to get his bearings. It just wouldn't sink in, that fateful moment when Nero twitched from the shock of the rifle bullet and went down. He shook his head.

Cavins ticked his horse's flanks with his spurs and started forward, up the slope.

"No," Dag whispered, drawing his pistol. "Don't go up there, Lonnie. That's what the bastard wants."

"Damn it, Dag!"

"Take a wide circle to the right. I'll circle left. Did you hear where the shot came from?"

"Way off to the left."

"That's what I thought. Horton is waiting up there, somewhere. He's hid out and he'll pick us both off if we show up top of that rise."

"Why don't I circle left with you, then? No use in me going right."

"You'll make a full circle and we might come at him from two sides. Watch yourself, hear?"

"I'll see you," Cavins said, and turned his horse to the right.

Dag let him get some distance before he backed Firefly down and started making his wide circle. He was breathing hard, his heart hammering in his chest. He choked back tears as he thought about Nero up on the hill, his beautiful mane rustling in the breeze, his tail flat and lifeless, fanned out on the ground like a stain.

What kind of a man could kill such a fine horse as Nero? Dag wondered. What kind of skunk? And for that matter, what kind of person could murder another human being for money? The lowest kind. Such a man did not deserve to live, but did he himself have the courage to take another's life? Even take life from a man like Horton?

Dag wrestled with these and other thoughts as he continued to circle where he thought Horton had been when he shot Nero. Then he started closing in on the ridge. He made a crucial decision while he still could see Nero's body up on the top of the slope. He holstered his pistol and slipped the heavy Henry Yellow Boy from its sheath, then eased out of the saddle.

He pointed Firefly toward the place where Nero's corpse lay and slapped its rump hard with the flat of his hand. The horse galloped off in that direction, scattering rocks and making a racket as it galloped away from him. He levered a cartridge into the chamber of the rifle and, hunched over, started running toward the top of the ridge.

When he cleared the ridge, Firefly was still on the run. That was when he saw the silhouette of a man rise up from the ground, holding a rifle in his hands. The man brought the rifle up to his shoulder and tracked the running horse.

"Horton," Dag yelled.

Horton turned in surprise and swung his rifle toward Dag.

"Drop it," Dag yelled.

The man fired straight at Dag, without hesitation. Dag ducked even more and heard the bullet sizzle the air like an angry hornet.

"You son of a bitch," Dag yelled as he stood up. He lined up the rear buckhorn sight with the front blade sight and squeezed the trigger. The butt of his rifle bucked against his shoulder.

Before Horton fell, Dag saw a puff of smoke, a belch of orange flame and felt a sledgehammer smash in his left shoulder. He spun around from the impact and saw clouds race by in a spiraling whirlwind. He pitched down and struck the ground. His rifle slipped from his hands and clattered on the rocks.

He heard a yell from somewhere as he fought against blackness and oblivion. He lay there, the breath knocked out of his lungs, and felt his head settle and his vision return. He reached out, grasped his rifle, and stood up.

"You got him, Dag," Cavins yelled. "You nailed the bastard."

Blood streamed from Dag's shoulder. He staggered toward the figure of Cavins standing over a dark shape on the ground. He squeezed his left arm against his rib cage, out of some instinct, perhaps, to stop the bleeding. He gritted his teeth against the pain that now seeped from his arm into his shoulder, down his back and up to his head.

He staggered up the rocky slope to where Cavins was standing over the body of Horton.

"You got hit?" Cavins asked.

"Yeah," Dag said, through clenched teeth.

"Let's have a look."

"Is he dead?"

"Plumb dead. You got him in the ticker, Dag."

Cavins laid his rifle down across Horton's legs. Horton's shirt was soaked with blood, but his heart was no longer pumping and flies boiled over the wound.

"You took a bullet in the arm," Cavins said, "but it went on through, kind of creasing you. Lot of blood and some ground-up meat, but he missed takin' your arm off or hittin' a big vein or such."

He untied the bandanna around his neck, shook it out, then folded it flat. He tied a tourniquet above the wound, knotted it, and then reached down and found a small stick, which he placed inside the knot. He tightened that, then took a couple of turns until the blood stopped gushing out.

"You're gettin' pale, Dag. We got to get you back and put some liniment and a proper bandage on you."

Dag's face was pale and he felt dizzy. The arm did not hurt so much now, but he was giddy, and a little bit addled. He looked around.

"Find his horse, Lonnie. We're packin' Horton back. Can you do that while I go over and pay my respects to Nero?"

"Sure, Dag," Cavins said quietly. "You go right ahead. I'll pack this piece of shit."

Dag looked up the hill and saw the hulk of Nero and started walking toward it. He laid his rifle down on the ground like a man bewildered, but going through the motions of life. The breeze was fresh and warm against his face, but it cooled the sweat that bathed his cheeks and forehead, that trickled down from under his hat.

Nero lay lifeless on the ground, his mane fluttering, his big brown eyes glassy and frosted over with the mist of death.

Dag knelt down and patted the horse's neck, bowed his head. He thought of all the rides he'd had with the animal, and the loyalty and trust Nero had shown him. His eyes misted over and he fought back tears as he ran his fingers through Nero's mane.

"You were a good horse, boy," he choked. "I hope you go to good pasture where the grass is high and green and have the company of your own kind. I am goin' to miss you, Nero boy, and I hope you miss me too."

Then Dag crumpled up and began to weep softly. After a minute, the sobs came from a deep place and he couldn't stop them. He put his head on Nero's neck and rubbed his back with soft strokes.

"Damn, it ain't right," Dag husked, and stood up, the sobs lessening now, some semblance of reason returning. He wiped his eyes with his shirtsleeve, closed them to squeeze out the last of the tears.

"So long, pard," he whispered, and the tears came back again, choking him, uncontrollably.

He looked up at the sky through wet eyes

and saw the clouds and the blue ocean and thought he heard Nero whinny from some far place, but it was only an illusion. The wind rose and blew against him. The scent of Nero wafted to his nostrils, not the scent of the dead horse, but the one that was still alive in his mind.

He did not look again at Nero, but started walking back down the slope, the wind at his back, and the acrid stench of death filling his nostrils and strangling his hammering heart.

Chapter 22

The delirium and the fever lasted three days. Dag lay on a makeshift cot inside the wagon that Finnerty had rigged for him. Fingers figured out that he could store food and utensils beneath the sickbed and not lose any space. Jo fed Dag hot and cold broth and wiped his feverish face with wet clothes while Dag raved or slept or hallucinated. It wasn't until after they had crossed Palo Duro Creek, a creek that had no connection with the canyon, that Dag started to come around. The wound in his arm had scabbed over and the broth helped him regain the blood he had lost.

The herd moved on, into New Mexico Territory.

For the past several weeks, Flagg had been training the herd not to stampede if it heard gunfire. He started out by having a man shoot one shot from his rifle at some distance from the herd. Each day, and always during the day, he ordered each shot to be fired closer to the herd. And for the past several days, the single shot had been fired within sight of the herd. The cattle had soon learned that they were not in danger from these odd noises.

Now Flagg wondered if the herd would stampede if a lot of rifles were fired and the animals were sent into a panic that caused them to run helter-skelter. He had been watching his backtrail and seeing the flash of mirrors. He had known, for a time, that they were being followed by Comanches, perhaps the same ones who had dogged them through Palo Duro Canyon.

Then the flashings had stopped, and he thought he knew why. The Comanches were closing in. The signaling had stopped shortly after they had burned Nero. The fire had sent a tall column of black smoke into the sky, which could be seen for many miles.

And he lied to Dag about that.

"What did you do with Nero?" Dag had asked during a lucid moment.

"We gave your horse a proper burial," Flagg said, "buried him deep to keep the critters from getting at him."

"Thanks, Jubal. What about Horton?"

"We stripped Horton naked and left his corpse on an anthill. I expect he's just bones by now."

And then Dag had drifted off again. But he remembered the conversation, because he thanked Flagg again.

"You won't believe what we found in Horton's boot, Dag."

"What?"

"It's almost like a signed confession. It's a contract between Deuce and Horton. Says if he murders you before we reach the Red, he gets your ranch and everything."

"That son of a bitch."

"You're going to have to deal with Deuce when you get back home, Dag. But you got proof enough to send him to the gallows. We'll all give testimony if there's a trial."

"There sure as hell's gonna be something," Dag said, a bitter tone to his voice.

Then the Comanches rose up out of nowhere, and they were everywhere, their faces painted for war, their arrows nocked on taut bowstrings, war clubs and lances piercing the skyline, tongues trilling, screams tearing from their throats.

"Look out," Manny Chavez yelled on the left flank where he was riding point.

Flagg turned in his saddle and saw them, their feathers rippling in the wind as the Comanche converged on lone riders at every manned point on the herd. He drew his rifle from his scabbard and turned his horse. He levered a cartridge into the chamber, cocking the rifle. He brought it to his shoulder and picked out the nearest target, a nearly naked Comanche, chest and face daubed in brilliant colors, loincloth flapping, charging Chavez with a lance. He led the running brave, squeezed the trigger and saw him fall as he launched his lance into the air.

Gunshots rang out as startled drovers drew pistols and rifles and picked out targets. Flagg saw men fall from their horses with arrows sprouting from their bodies. He swung his rifle, dropped another Comanche, and then three of them came after him. He put spurs to his horse's flanks and charged straight at them, firing once, swerving his horse, jerking the lever down, then back up and swerving again as arrows whistled through the air, then whispered past him, only to strike the ground and chip sparks from rocks or impale the ground at an angle, the shafts vibrating with a brittle hum.

A brave dragged a man from his horse. Another ran up and swung a war club. The club struck the man in the side of the head and smashed it like a ripe pumpkin, scattering brains and blood like boiled oatmeal streaked with ketchup. A drover riding drag took a Comanche arrow in the belly and screamed. Two warriors came at him on moccasined feet, slashing with war clubs. The rider swung his rifle at them, but the clubs smashed his kneecaps and shins. Ed Langley screamed in pain as he was dragged out of the saddle and brained until his face looked like a distorted mask floating at the bottom of a vat of water.

Jimmy Gough left Little Jake in charge of the remuda and rode to the rear of the herd, his rifle cocked. He shot on the run, dropping one Comanche, jacking another cartridge into the chamber and squeezing the trigger on another who was trying to kill one of the drovers with his lance.

Fingers and Jo halted the chuck wagon at the sound of rifle shots. But they were out of sight of the herd and could not see what was happening. Fingers turned the wagon broadside to the trail.

"Jo, hand me that Henry under the seat," he said. "You grab the Greener and watch in case somebody comes after us."

"Daddy, it sounds like the drovers are under attack." She handed her father the rifle and put the shotgun on her lap.

Dag rose up in the back as the wagon was turning. He had been asleep. "Wha-what is it?" he asked, still groggy and thick-tongued.

"Felix, you lie still now, hear?" Jo said. "We're just turning the wagon."

"I hear shots."

"I know. There's nothing we can do about it. Now hush."

Dag laid his head back down, realizing how weak he was. Just that small effort had put a sheen of sweat on his face, and brought back the throbbing pain in his arm.

The gunfire continued, fast and furious,

sounding like the crack of whips in rapid succession.

Flagg saw them coming and swung his rifle on them. But at the same time, he saw a Comanche warrior drawing his bow back, aiming an arrow at him.

A dozen or more Indians came boiling over the ridge, leading an equal number of riderless horses, each to a man. The pack of charging warriors broke into single riders, who rode for the fighting men on the ground, picking them up one by one.

Flagg fired quickly, just as the Comanche loosed his arrow, then ducked. He saw the man jerk with the impact of a bullet just below his gullet, then collapse to the ground, blood spurting from his throat.

He swung his rifle toward the pack of Comanches, but by then they were split up. He saw what was happening. As each man on foot leaped on the back of a horse, the Comanches began cutting cattle out of the herd. They all converged and drove the stolen cattle off, yipping and screeching to keep them running away from the herd.

Flagg had never seen such horsemanship before. All of the Comanches were now mounted and weaving their ponies back and forth, herding the cattle perfectly while on the run. He fired a shot at one of the Indians, but it went high and wide.

And then the Comanches were gone, along with about a dozen head of cattle.

Matlee rode up, his face covered with sweat and dust. "Jubal, we goin' after 'em?"

"Barry, there could be a hundred Indians just over that hill yonder, just waitin' for us. Do you figger it's worth it?"

"Hell, they stole our cattle. A couple of hundred dollars' worth, at least."

Flagg looked around. Men were moaning, lying flat on their backs or doubled up in pain. There were dead Comanches too. Riderless horses, under saddle, wandered in confusion. The cattle were bawling and milling, as if ready to bolt.

"This herd could jump at any minute, Barry. Let's tend to what we got."

Matlee scowled, but nodded, and turned his horse. "I got men down," he said.

Flagg watched the dust hanging in the air, left by the retreating Comanches. He knew it was not worth the risk to go after the thieves when there was a chance they could lose the entire herd and spend days tracking the cattle down.

He waited until the dust dissipated and then reloaded his rifle, shoved it into its boot. He turned to the herd, saw that some men were tending to the wounded, while others were trying to calm the herd and keep them from stampeding.

"Manny, let's string 'em out," Flagg said. "Keep 'em movin' ahead. Don't give 'em time to think."

"Yeah, boss," Chavez said. He and the two riders from the Double C started cutting through the head of the herd, sending small bunches of cattle after the lead steer and the bunch following it into the stream heading northwest.

Flagg watched the herd for any sign of revolt, barking orders, holding the strays in, helping where he could. Soon the herd was strung out and moving at a good pace, settling down, following blindly behind the cattle in the lead.

"Manny, you let 'em graze when you think they're ready. I'll have riders keep an eye on our back trail. The drovers are set."

Chavez nodded as Flagg rode up to Jimmy.

"They drive off any horses?" Flagg asked.

"I don't know. I left Little Jake to watch the remuda."

"Let's find out," Flagg said.

Little Jake's face was drained of color. He had an old cap-and-ball pistol in his hand and it was shaking as if he had the palsy.

"Lose any horseflesh, Little Jake?" Gough asked.

"Nary a one, Jimmy. I didn't even see one Comanche come near. But I was ready to shoot if one did."

"Good man, Little Jake," Flagg said. "Now put that pistol away before you shoot one of the horses in the ass."

"Yes, sir," Bogel said, only too glad to finally be told what to do.

"And when you get paid, get yourself a good Colt and throw that one away," Flagg said, "or use it for a sashweight when you build yourself a house."

"It's been a right good pistol, Mr. Flagg."

"And so was the sword in its time, son."

Jimmy chuckled. Little Jake looked puzzled as he holstered the black powder weapon, an 1851 Navy Colt.

"Golly, Jimmy," Little Jake Bogel said, "Mr. Flagg talked to me."

"Just hope he don't talk to you when he's got a burr under his blanket."

Then Jimmy saw men carrying the dead to a little hill alongside the trail. Tears stung his eyes and he had to take deep breaths to keep from getting sick to his stomach.

Little Jake leaned out from the saddle and emptied his breakfast onto the lone prairie as buzzards appeared out of nowhere and made lazy circles in the sky.

really, with the two Double C men, but all of them felt the loss of those six men keenly and deeply, as if part of their lives had been torn away from them, leaving them hollow inside, with the faces of the dead fading from memory at the end of each passing day.

And Dag remembered Fingers taking him from the wagon when he was so sick, to relieve himself and crying out for Laura in his delirium for a time, until he only called out for Jo, and Laura's face was fading too. When he tried to think of her, her face would change and he would see only Jo's and he cursed his memory and himself for being so faithless. But Jo had been his ministering angel, and when he saw her bending over him, in the soft twilight, spooning hot broth into his mouth, he wanted to draw her to him and hold her tight and run his fingers through her hair and kiss that little rosebud of a mouth and make it flower.

The wound had changed him, Dag reasoned. He would return to his true nature one day. Maybe when the drive was over, or when he was back home with Laura and their little baby. The place where the bullet had furrowed through his flesh had long since healed and he had full use of his arm. Once in a while, if he moved it in a certain way, he would feel a slight twinge, but he didn't know if it was real or only his skin's memory, like a man with an amputated foot would feel his toes wriggle when there were no toes there anymore.

They had passed the little town of Conchas, where they stocked up on supplies, and were now at the swollen Mora River, where they had been waiting two days to find a ford to cross. Dag was searching for a ford now, without finding any place shallow enough to risk putting cattle into without putting them and the drovers in danger. He rode back to where the herd was bunched, to see if anyone else had found a suitable ford.

"The water isn't going down none," Flagg said, "and it looks like we're going to get more rain. Look at that sky to the west."

Dag saw the black thunderheads gathering over the mountains, heading their way slowly. He shook his head.

"We've been here two days, Jubal," he said.

"And we could be here a week. Dag, I'm going to send some of the men back. We can't afford to keep 'em on the payroll. Fingers is strapped for supplies until we get to the next town."

"We stocked up in Conchas."

"Some of the food was plumb spoiled," Flagg said.

"Shit."

"Who do you want to send back?"

Dag thought for a moment. He looked at the men, many of whom had started to grumble, and the night before, some of his hands got into a fracas with some Box M drovers. Fists flew and blood was spilled. Hard feelings remained.

"How many?" Dag asked.

"We only need a dozen men at most to finish the drive. Maybe fifteen."

"I think we'll need fifteen, at least."

"Make your choice, Dag."

Dag drew a deep breath. "We can send Chad Myers back. He's got a family that's probably hurtin' by now. And Carl Costello. Ricardo Mendoza, maybe. That's about all I could spare."

"All right. Matlee will send a couple or three back. I think you're keeping the best hands, Dag."

"Thanks."

But it was a tough decision. Over the miles,

he had drawn very close to not only his men, but to Matlee's. And the two hands from the Double C were working out fine. They had a good crew.

Vince Sutphen, one of the two Double C hands, rode up from the east.

"I think I found a place to ford," he told Flagg.

"Show me," Flagg said.

Dag followed them downriver, past an oxbow, to a place where the river widened. He could see riffles showing that it was more shallow there than up above.

"Did you try it?" Flagg asked.

Sutphen shook his head.

"Well, head on into it, Vince. Take your time."

Dag and Jubal watched as Sutphen put his horse in at a point where the bank was low. His horse stepped out gingerly, eyes rolling in their sockets showing more white than brown. The water came up to the horse's knees just off the bank, but on firmer footing, the water was only ankle deep. Sutphen turned his horse halfway across and rode toward the hollow of the bend, stepping off gravel in the shallows. The water was belly deep for a few yards; then he was again in shallow water, clear to the opposite bank.

"Good enough," Flagg said.

"Water's awful swift," Sutphen said. "My horse liked to have went down there a couple of times. I had to hold him against the current. Was a cow to founder, she'd be carried off."

Flagg looked downstream. The river narrowed and the water roared just beyond the ford, rushing between its banks.

"All right, Vince. Come on back and see how it goes," Flagg said. He turned to Dag. "We're still droppin' calves," he said. "Wolves carried off two last night, but we still got a passel of 'em."

"I know," Dag said. "They'd never get across here on their own."

"We'll have to carry 'em acrost," Flagg said.

"Then we will."

Sutphen had to fight the current coming back over a slightly different course. They could see the horse wobble and falter, slip and almost fall. In the deep part, the horse had to swim and it lost ground, but recovered, just barely, before it was swept away downstream.

"'At's a son of a bitch in parts," Sutphen

said, when he put his horse back up on the bank. "We'll have to be mighty careful."

"Maybe we should wait another day," Dag said.

Flagg shook his head, looking off to the northwest.

"Nope, we got to get 'em acrost today, Dag. And mighty quick. That storm's a comin' and it'll be a frog strangler. Rain'll come down like a cow pissin' on a flat rock."

They rode back and Flagg took over, ordering the drovers to turn the herd downriver. At the ford, he told Chavez to pick out two men to send downstream.

"Two good ropers, Manny. We're going to have some cows get away from us and I want them to drag 'em out."

"What about the little ones?" Chavez asked.

"We'll all have to carry those calves across. I don't want to lose a single one." He pointed straight up at the sky. Buzzards were gathering like undertakers at a massacre.

Chavez nodded.

"You take the lead steer across, Manny, and the rest ought to follow. We may have to whip some of 'em into the river."

While Flagg and Dagstaff led the chuck

wagon across, holding on to the traces of the mules, the drovers turned the herd, moving them slowly down to the ford. Chavez sent Skip Hughes and Barry Matlee downstream with extra lariats to catch any cattle that washed their way. The wagon made it across at a very slow pace, but rumbled out on the other bank and up onto dry land, then proceeded on to the northwest at a lumbering pace.

Next, Chavez ordered Jimmy and Little Jake to run the remuda across, watching the progress of the stock and letting the cows watch, as well. The lead steer stood there, its forelegs extended and stiffened, showing Manny that he didn't want to go anywhere near that rushing water.

"Ready, Jubal," Chavez said, when all the horses were across and well out of the way.

"Dag, you come right on in after I get that lead steer in the water," Flagg said. "Manny, you and your boys be ready to crowd 'em."

When all hands were set, Flagg roped the lead steer, rode into the water, and pulled the steer in as Dag pushed with Firefly from the rear.

Once the cattle started into the water, those on the shore started bawling. Cows struggled against the current and one started to wash away, regained its footing, and continued on. It took hours to get the herd across and some did get swept downstream. Each drover picked up a calf and carried those across via a slightly different route. Dag carried five calves across himself.

Cowhands kept crowding the herd so that they became a steady stream fording the swift waters. In the west, the clouds moved closer and the sky overhead became overcast, then began to darken. By the time the entire herd had reached the opposite bank, it was late afternoon and looked like dusk.

The hands downstream had lost only five head, but they rescued more than a dozen and brought them back, and dragged them over with ropes around the bosses of the longhorns.

Dag was riding drag with the other late-crossing hands when the first raindrops began to spatter his face.

Then the temperature dropped sharply, and the wind picked up to a brisk thirty knots, gusting to forty or more. Riders slipped into their slickers and pulled down their hats.

A few moments later, it started to hail with a sudden ferocity. Pea-sized hailstones pelted

Dag and the other riders, stinging their faces, chests, and arms. Then the hailstones grew larger until they were the size of walnuts. It grew sharply colder and the wind howled over the land with whipping and swirling gusts.

Dag could barely see twenty yards ahead and then his visibility dropped to less than ten feet, then to five. He heard a roar up ahead and the terrible sound of thousands of cattle bawling. He spurred Firefly ahead, ducking to avoid the steady blows of hailstones on his face. He saw, finally, the herd moving away from him in a full run, and out of the corners of his eyes, he saw cattle streaming out of the herd and disappearing into the rain, the hail, and the churned-up mist from the damp ground.

"Stampede," Dag yelled, but there was no one to hear him. When he looked around, he saw none of the drag riders. The hailstones grew larger and he was nearly knocked senseless by one the size of a pear that struck him in the head. Another smashed into his cheek, drawing blood where it had cracked the skin.

Dag lost all sense of direction. He could feel the ground tremble beneath Firefly's hooves when he stopped and hunkered down to escape the brunt of the wind's blast and hurtling onslaught of lethal hailstones.

His heart pounded as the rumbling sound subsided and there was only the clatter of icy balls of hail striking the ground, smashing into rocks. Firefly quivered beneath him, his head hanging low, helpless against the cannonballs that struck his wet hide and staggered him nearly to his knees.

Dag writhed as each stone struck him, bringing a stinging pain, not only to his flesh, but his bones.

And worst of all, he thought, he was completely lost, with the precious herd in full stampede.

Chapter 24

The ground was white and cold when the hail stopped. Dag saw dead jackrabbits lying here and there, stoned to death by the rocketing hail. Now a steady chill rain fell. Dag pulled his sougan free of its lashing behind the cantle and slipped into it. His was a heavy poncho that he wished he'd had when the storm started. He was cold, shivering, and soaked through to the skin as he started trying to pick up the trail of at least some of the cattle that had scattered to the winds.

As he rode, without bearings, ducking his head against the slashing rain, Dag saw a dead quail, then another, and the icy hail melting ever so slowly, for the rain was almost as cold as the ice that blanketed the ground. He heard an unearthly sound, and he rode toward it. As he drew closer, he realized it was a calf, and it was bawling at the top of its lungs. He came upon it, saw it standing there, shivering and shaking on wobbly little legs, as forlorn a sight as he'd ever seen.

The calf did not move when Dag rode up. He dismounted, picked it up in his arms. It struggled feebly as he mounted Firefly, and when he was in the saddle, he pulled the sougan over it to protect it from the rain, keep it warm against his own shivering body. He rode on, blindly, listening for sounds beneath the patter of rain, the heavy sighing of the wind.

More dead quail. And rabbits. A manzanita bush fractured and smashed, its skeleton filled with balls of hail. Then a roadrunner sprawled out, brained, in a rivulet of water where the hail had melted, its wing and tail feathers rippling from the flow of water. A young antelope limped along, bleating softly, one of its legs broken. It did not run away when Dag rode right up on it. He felt sorry for the small creature. A wolf or a coyote would have it for supper sometime during the night.

That was the way of nature, he knew. It was

not cruel, merely unfeeling, dispassionate. It gave and it took away. It let things be what they would be. It let things happen that would happen without judgment or criticism. He sighed and rode on, coming then upon cows huddling together in clusters or singly, their rumps pointed toward the wind, their heads, with their long sweeping horns, hanging disconsolately. He left them as they were, for he did not know in which direction to drive them and they were not going anywhere for a while.

He hoped the stampede was over, and he heard nothing to prove that any cattle were still in a mad run, gripped in fear, blind to all but the panic that flowed through a herd at such times like an electric charge.

A rattlesnake swam ahead of him over the icy ground and the tiny waterways, while another lay dead, its head smashed flat, its tail quivering as if life still clung to it in some mysterious way. *The quick and the dead*, Dag thought, and continued on, looking for the road he had ridden the year before.

The road loomed before him, an ancient buffalo trail that he knew to be one of the highways of the West. *The trail*, he thought. And somewhere in the mix of the pattering rain and the slosh of the melting ice, he heard cattle lowing, grumbling deep in their chests and he headed Firefly toward the sound. The calf had settled down and only quivered sporadically, so, his arm nearly numb, he scooted his butt back up the cantle and let the calf gently down on the saddle, between the pommel and his lap, where it draped like some dead furry thing.

Past dismembered and bleeding cactus he rode, struggling to see through the rain that peppered his face, stung his eyes. A figure loomed up in the silver-sheeted darkness, a man on horseback, dark-cloaked behind a shimmering wall of rain, his horse's legs enveloped in a fine mist, its hocks spattered with dripping mud.

"Who's there?" Dag called, as he approached.

"That you, Mr. Dagstaff?" It was Skip Hughes, his massive bulk seeming small inside his black slicker, the brim of his hat sogged downward like a wilting flower.

"Yeah, Skip. That the herd beyond you?"

Hughes laughed harshly, a wry tone to it that made it humorless.

"What's left of it, I reckon. Me'n some of the boys are holding these."

"How many?"

"Maybe a thousand head or so. Hard to tell in this rain. Hell, you can't see ten feet."

Dag looked over a sea of spiked horns sprouting upward like naked trees in a dead forest. Visibility was more like twenty yards, but it was sporadic, as the wind gusted and lashed at them, rattling their raincoats with a tinny tattoo.

"They got a fire goin' up ahead," Hughes said. "Up against a big rock. Chuck wagon's there, with a broken spoke. Whatcha got under your sougan, Mr. Dagstaff?"

"Lost calf."

"Imagine we might have lost a few of the young 'uns," Hughes said.

Dag said nothing. He rode off into the needling rain and the darkness, following the contours of the bunched herd, passing men on horseback hunched down in their slickers like deformed creatures recently emerged from Dante's Hell. None of them spoke to him and he did not speak to them.

There were other, smaller bunches of cattle

packed together, their rumps to the wind and the slashing, needling rain, silent wraiths, still shivering from the cold and beaten into submission by the recent hail.

Dag saw the fire then, reflecting off a rock wall that was part of an outcropping risen up from the harsh land centuries ago. Then the wagon, part of it lit by a storm lantern flickering an orange light, swaying back and forth as if someone were signaling a passing train.

Jo was holding the storm lantern, while her father was wrestling with a wheel, trying to put in a new wooden spoke, his dark hulk hunched over the sawhorses, a small maul in his hand.

Jo was wearing overalls and a yellow slicker that glistened like wet butter in the lantern light.

Flagg came up on foot, away from the fire. "Dag," he said.

"Jubal, take this little calf, will you? Put him by the fire. He's shiverin' like a dog shittin' peach seeds."

Dag lifted his sougan and Flagg reached for the calf, lifted it tenderly out of the crotch of the saddle.

"Hey there, little feller," Flagg said. "We'll get you warm right quick."

Dag stepped out of the saddle, tied Firefly to the front of the wagon, behind the wet and disconsolate mules still hooked to it like beaten dogs to a stone sledge too heavy to pull.

"Fingers, can I help?" Dag asked when he walked around to the other side of the wagon. "Jo?"

"I'm fine," Jo said.

"You can tilt this wheel a mite," Fingers said. "I 'bout got it, I think."

Dag grabbed one side of the ironclad wheel and tilted it upward. Fingers slid one end of the wheel into a hole in the hub. The wood groaned as he pushed it in, then made a small snapping sound as it slid in and snugged up.

"Set the wheel down, Dag," Fingers said. "Upright. I just want to tap the rim some to make sure she's snug."

Dag set the wheel down, slid his hands to the sides. Fingers took the hand maul and tapped on the upper rim.

"Snug as a bug," he said.

Together, Dag and Fingers rolled the wheel over to the wagon. The rear end was jacked up, the bed resting on a boulder. They slid the wheel onto the axle and Fingers tapped in the peg that kept the wheel on, and slipped the thong over a flange on the wheel hub, so that if it ever slipped out, it would not be lost.

Jo let the lantern down, then shifted it to her other hand and rubbed the arm that had carried its weight.

"Should I put out the lantern, Daddy?" Jo asked.

"Naw, not yet. Hang it up on that hook underneath the bed."

"What happened?" Dag asked.

"Wagon hit a big hole and we dropped a foot or so and hit a big old rock. Splintered one spoke." He reached down and picked up the broken spoke to show it to Dag. "We was lucky, Dag. The wagon pitched and I thought we were going to go over. Me'n Jo shifted our weight and righted it. Just in time."

Dag looked at Jo. She looked so forlorn with her rain-splashed face and hair streaming down around it like sodden black crepe. She was shivering.

"Let's go over by the fire, Jo," Dag said. "I'm some cold too."

"Y-y-yes," she stuttered. "I'm plumb froze

through." Then she laughed and Dag put an arm around her back and they walked to the blazing fire, Fingers following in their wake.

The rock reflected the heat toward them and Jo soon stopped shivering. The little calf was standing there, bleating pitifully like a little lost lamb, with Flagg's hand stroking its back.

"Oh, Dag," Jo said. "You saved the little tyke. He's so cute."

"He's a heifer," Dag chided. "She's cold and hungry."

"And I can't feed her," Jo said. "We need to find her mama."

They stood there as riders came in and those who were warm left to relieve them. Dag rubbed his hands to bring back the circulation. His fingers were wrinkled and bone white at the tips, like some unknown vegetable preserved in brine.

The rain lessened, finally, but it was still cold.

"Never saw a colder rain," Flagg said, "nor so much of it all at once't."

Dag nodded. He was thinking about the stampede. No one had mentioned it, as if bringing it up just then would be taboo. But he knew Flagg was thinking about the scattered cattle as well.

"Not all the cattle are scattered," Dag said, after a few moments, turning his back to the fire. Someone—he didn't know who—was putting more deadwood on it. "I passed Skip, who was with about a thousand head."

"Dag, there's near three thousand more we've got to get back when we can see our hands in front of our faces. I wish this damned rain would stop."

"It will," Dag said. "They won't run any more tonight and we can start roundup in the morning when the sun comes up."

"Yeah, it's going to be a damned mess," Flagg said. "And we'll likely lose or never find a few."

As if to emphasize Flagg's dire prediction, a wolf howled from a long way off, its mournful cry so depressing, nobody by the fire even mentioned it. But they all shivered, not from the cold, but from the dread of what they might find in the morning. Jo huddled against Dag and he put an arm around her. She looked up at him in gratitude and smiled a weak smile, the rosebud of her lips faded to a pale bloodless remnant.

He wanted her at that moment so badly, he could taste those lips that he dared not kiss.

Chapter 25

Haggard, sleep-deprived drovers and cow-hands roamed the desolate countryside, rounding up strays, searching for lost cattle. They found some dead calves, disemboweled, half-eaten by wolves, scavenged by coyotes, and now fed upon by turkey buzzards drawn to the smell of death.

Flagg told Dag that, near as he could tell, the stampeding cattle had not run more than three miles in a more or less straight line. However, there were cattle scattered all over the land on both sides of the old buffalo trail.

"How long do you figure getting 'em all back will take?" Dag asked.

"Two days ought to do it. But we won't get

'em all back, Dag. My men have already had to shoot two steers with busted legs, and we've found at least five or six calves that didn't make it. I'm just fearful that some of 'em might have wandered into the Canadian during the night. It's runnin' worse than that damned Mora."

"I know. I heard it roar all night. It's too bad we had to cross there, where the Mora feeds into the Canadian, but we couldn't drive around it. Anyways, I don't know how far the Mora runs west."

"I don't pay that crossing no nevermind now, Dag. We got across before it got too bad. We were lucky."

"Yeah."

When Hughes and the others brought up the cattle they had guarded during the night, Dag turned the calf he had saved into the herd. It soon found a mother, or its mother, and had suckled in the warmth of the morning sun, butting its head against the bag to squeeze as much milk as it could from her teats.

Flagg sent the chuck wagon ahead and started the herd moving, what there was of it. He rode point and told the drovers to just bunch up the runaways they caught and then follow him. It was, he told them, going to be a long day, but he wanted every head brought in. "Even if you have to make a dozen gathers."

By late afternoon, the herd had swollen to almost its previous number. A couple of drovers told about cattle with broken legs that they'd had to shoot. Flagg told Chavez to get a couple of hands and give him a head count. The chuck wagon had not stopped for lunch, but hands picked up hardtack and beef jerky, and ate in the saddle as the main herd moved north and west, following the trail Dag had marked off for them the previous year.

Over the next several days, following along the west bank of the Canadian River, the drive reached a small, nameless settlement, an Indian trading post, where most of the hands got shaves and haircuts, losing their ferocious mountain man looks, and a few got mildly drunk and suffered the consequences as the herd moved on. Fingers was able to buy rice and beans and twenty pounds of coffee, which made him feel better. Jo braided her long dark hair into a single comely braid, and to Dag, she looked prettier than ever.

It was hard work driving the herd over

Raton Pass and into Colorado, but they finally reached Pueblo, marveling, as they drove north to Denver, at the towering Rocky Mountains, many of which were still capped with snow in a breathless display of majesty such as none but Dag had ever seen before. They watered the herd in Cherry Creek and picked up a crowd of onlookers when they drove through Denver. Several buyers approached Dag and Matlee in Denver, offering to pay twenty-five dollars a head if they would run a thousand head into the stockyards.

Matlee wanted to sell his brand there and go back home, figuring that was enough profit for him.

"Barry, we have an agreement," Dag said. "You know if you pull out here, I'll lose my deal in Cheyenne."

"My hands are plumb worn down to a nub-bin, Dag. You could maybe sell all of your stock here and still go back home and pay off your mortgage with Deuce."

"And break my word to Jim Bellaugh and the Rocky Mountain Cattleman's Association. Nobody would ever trust me again."

"You sure ain't thinkin' to drive another herd up this way, Dag."

"I might."

"You're plumb loco, son. This drive has been enough punishment for all of us, 'specially you."

"A man's word is a man's word, Barry. I put a high price on mine."

"Damn it, Dag, so do I. But a man has to be on the lookout for opportunity and we got one here."

Flagg was listening to the argument and he never said a word until it was just about over.

"Barry," he said, "it might be none of my business, but you got a good long life ahead of you. If you sell out your partner, the deed will foller you all your life."

Dag looked at Flagg in admiration. "Thanks for backin' me up, Jubal," he said.

"I ain't doin' it for you, Dag, but for Barry here. He's thinkin' of makin' a big mistake."

"Gangin' up on me, are you? Well, I've a good mind to sell my seven hundred head and ride on back."

"And what are you going to do with the money, Barry?" Dag asked. "Buy more land? Buy more stock? And if you do either, how will that help? Ain't a rancher in Texas would help you fix a broken pump or a windmill.

Ain't a drover who will work for you. Ain't a buyer will buy from you. You'll wind up eatin' dirt and that's for damned sure."

"All right, boys," Matlee said, finally, "you win. I'll keep my end of the agreement. We go on to Cheyenne. I just hope the offer with Bellaugh still stands."

And that was just what Dag was thinking when they left Denver and its temptations. But all the drovers had gotten some rest and some of them had gotten properly drunk, and some had played with the glitter gals and lost money at cards in the saloons and gambling dens on Larimer Street.

From Denver, they journeyed north along the South Platte, laying over a while at Fort Collins, then on to the old Cheyenne Trail. The cattle had fattened on the drive and the calves born along the way—those that survived the weather, floods, and storms and that weren't cooked up by Fingers—had good legs under them and seemed to be thriving.

A number of stray curs followed the herd out of Denver. Jimmy Gough and Little Jake had the task of shooing them away, but they didn't see the last of the dogs until they were almost where the Cache de la Poudre River emptied into the South Platte at La Porte.

They entered the Sweetwater Valley and bedded the herd down just outside Cheyenne. Dag, Matlee, and Flagg rode into town and checked into the Becker Hotel, where Dag arranged for a man to ride out to the 3 Bar 8 Ranch and tell Bellaugh that he was there with the herd. Word had already spread, however, and many of the townspeople, curious, rode out to look at the herd and meet the cowboys who had driven the animals all the way up from Texas. They all marveled at the size of the herd and the quality of the animals. They met the drovers and cowhands and asked a lot of questions. Some of them showed their hospitality by extending invitations to supper or to church.

James Bellaugh was a tall, rangy man with a small handlebar mustache. He found the trio from Texas in the dining room. By then, Dag, Jubal, and Barry had bathed, shaved, and changed clothes. They looked somewhat presentable for men who had driven a large herd of cattle more than a thousand miles.

Bellaugh smiled and shook their hands. "I've

seen the herd, Mr. Dagstaff," Bellaugh said. "I've got a man grading them and making the tally even as we speak."

"That's fine, Mr. Bellaugh," Dag said. "Does your offer depend on the grade, then?"

"Not particularly. But I want to know what I'm buying."

"Are you going to raise the cattle yourself or resell them?"

Bellaugh lifted a hand to summon a waiter whose eye he had caught. "First, a little whiskey," Bellaugh said, "and then we'll talk business."

Bellaugh ordered a whiskey from the waiter and then turned back to the men at the table.

"How many head did you arrive with, Mr. Dagstaff?"

"Purt near four thousand steers and cows. Some calves."

"I contracted for less than that."

"Yes, you did."

"Depending on the tally, I'll take them all. You throw in the calves. I'll use those for breeding stock, maybe."

"Fair enough."

"Forty dollars a head," Bellaugh said. He took a sip of his whiskey.

"Forty-five," Dag said. "That was the price we agreed on."

"For prime stock, yes."

"Far as I'm concerned, the whole herd is prime stock."

"Forty-five, then." Bellaugh extended his arm across the table and the two men shook hands.

The waiter brought plates of food for Dag, Matlee, and Flagg. The three men tucked into the food. Dag heard something crinkle. He looked up and Bellaugh was holding an envelope in his hand.

"Almost forgot," he said. "This came for you yesterday, Mr. Dagstaff."

Dag reared back in surprise. "For me?"

"Yes, sir. It's addressed to you in care of me."

"Yeah, I left your address with my wife before I left."

Bellaugh handed the letter across the table.

Dag looked at the return address. "It ain't from my wife," he said, his voice heavy with dread.

"Open it, Dag," Flagg said. "Might be good news. Wasn't your woman expectin' a baby?"

"It's way too soon, Jubal."

Dag looked at the name on the return address. It was from Carmelita Delgado, the woman who was watching after Laura. He opened the envelope. The letter from Carmelita was in Spanish, but he knew the language.

Muy estimado Felix, read the formal greeting. Then he read the first line and his heart squeezed tight in his chest.

Quanto lamento lo que ha pasado, the letter began. "I'm so sorry for what has happened."

Tears began to flow down Dag's cheeks as he read the rest of it. He read it again and more tears flowed from his eyes. He looked up at Flagg and Matlee.

"Laura's—Laura's dead," he said. "She had a miscarriage and lost the baby. They—they couldn't stop the bleeding."

"I'm sorry, Dag," Flagg said softly.

"My sympathies, Dag," Matlee said. "I'm awful sorry."

"Mr. Dagstaff," Bellaugh said, "please accept my condolences and my deepest sympathies."

But Dag didn't hear them. He thought of Laura dying all alone, but he could not yet believe it. He could see her face now, shining, glowing with the life that had been inside her. He heard her voice and her laughter and he smelled her fragrance, felt the softness of her hair when she brushed her face against his cheek.

He took a deep breath and wiped the tears from his face.

Then, he just sat there, staring back through time, thinking of the day he had left Laura to ride north with the herd. He thought of their last kiss and her arms around him, squeezing him, her breasts burning into his chest.

"I ain't hungry no more," he said, numbly. "I think I'll have one of those whiskies."

But the liquor didn't take away any of the pain; it only deepened his sadness.

enne, and she grew more beautiful, Dag thought, with each day's passing.

They stopped over in Pueblo, homesick for Mexican food, then continued on over Raton Pass and into New Mexico, with the larder in the chuck wagon full. Some of them had taken scatterguns up on the Colorado prairie and shot game: doves streaking south for Mexico, prairie chickens, and top-knotted quail such as none he had seen before.

They rode through the gathering chill of New Mexico, followed the Canadian, crossed the Mora, and felt butterflies in their stomachs as they neared Texas. They knew they were making better time than they had on the drive up to Cheyenne. Jimmy had sold off some of the horses in Cheyenne, so the remuda had shrunk considerably. All of the hands, including Dag, switched horses daily, so that they always had a fresh mount each morning.

Flagg had been offered a job by James Bellaugh, but he had turned the offer down. Bellaugh had warned them of thieves who might attack them and rob them when they left Cheyenne, and while they had seen a few suspicious riders, none had attacked them. There was safety in numbers, Matlee kept saying, which showed Dag just how scared he was of being robbed.

A few times, Indians trailed them, but a show of rifles soon left them in the dust and they encountered none brave enough to sound the war cry.

Dag felt hollow inside, the emptiness filled with an unutterable sadness that his Laura was dead and that he would be going back to an empty house. His mind was full of memories and they crept into his dreams each night.

Jo tried her best to comfort Dag without imposing upon his grief or intruding into his private thoughts. But she was grieving too, not only for Laura, but for Dag, who seemed to be trying to avoid being alone with her.

They crossed into Texas and headed southeast. The two drovers from the Double C said their farewells and took the money Dag gave them and thanked him profusely. They were good men, he knew, and perfectly trustworthy.

"You say howdy to Gus and Janet, hear?" Dag said, just before they rode off.

"Y'all come back," Tom Leeds said, with a tip of his hat.

"Y'all are always welcome at the Double C," Sutphen said.

Dag watched them go and there was a sadness in that parting too.

Into the warmth of Texas, they rode, and down the Palo Duro Canyon with its striated colors painted brilliant by the sun, and the smell of Texas full in their nostrils with each passing day, long days when their pace quickened. *Heading for home,* Dag thought, and the emptiness inside him would leave him with that hollow feeling and more memories of Laura.

"Felix, what are you going to do when you get back?" Jo asked when they were sitting by a stream, eating a basket lunch she had packed for just the two of them.

"I guess I'll grieve some more for poor Laura," he said, "and then get to goin' on best I can."

"I'm so sorry. I know you're hurting real bad inside."

"I can't really talk about it, Jo."

"Someday you'll have to, Felix."

"Just not now," he said, and they ate their sliced beef sandwiches and drank wine Fingers had bought in Cheyenne.

"I understand," she said, "but if you need me or Daddy, you just holler, hear?"

"I will," he said, and hated himself for being so distant, so cold.

And maybe, he thought, he hated himself for flirting with Jo on the drive up to Cheyenne. Maybe he also hated himself for harboring thoughts of infidelity with Jo on those nights when he ached for Laura, when he wanted to hold his wife in his arms and make love to her. Tender, sweet Jo, a beautiful woman in season, but forbidden by his strict moral code.

And then they were home, and more farewells sounded as Matlee and his men rode to the Box M, and Dag continued on to the D Slash.

"You be careful, old timer," Flagg said, as he shook hands with Dag. "Don't take no wooden nickels."

"You too, Jubal. It was quite a ride."

Flagg let fly a stream of tobacco juice and shifted the cud in his mouth from one cheek to the other.

"I never had so much fun since the hogs ate my baby brother," Flagg joked.

"You got us through it, Jubal."

"I reckon you had a strong hand in it, Dag."

It was awkward after that, and Jubal Flagg rode off to his home, where he had no woman waiting for him, just a house and creek and horses.

Jimmy and Little Jake said goodbye and rode off with the rest of the remuda, which had dwindled to a few head as each hand took his own horses and left for their homes.

Finally, there were only Dag, Fingers, and Jo.

"We'll ride up to home with you, Dag," Fingers said. "See if you need anything before we head for home."

"You don't have to do that, Fingers."

"It's on our way."

Jo got down from the wagon and walked up to the silent house with Dag. She put her arm inside one of his and he crooked it and held it close to his side.

"Don't fight me, Felix, please," she said, as they stood at the porch steps. "I'm not your enemy."

He looked at her, patted her hand, then released her arm.

"I know, Jo. I just ain't myself is all."

"It's going to be hard walking in there," she said.

"I reckon I'm glad to be home. I just feel awful tired all of a sudden. I think I need to sleep for a week."

"We all do," she said, smiling. She patted his hand, and he did not draw it away.

"You take care, Jo," he said, and put a boot up on the first step.

"Don't be a stranger, Felix. You know I care for you."

"I won't. And I know you do. I care for you too, I reckon."

She stood on tiptoe and pecked his lips with a brief kiss. Then she turned and walked away. Dag watched her climb back up on the wagon. Fingers waved to him and he waved back. Jo turned and raised a hand. She moved it in a disconsolate wave and then bowed her head and turned it away from him.

Dag knew she was starting to cry and that was a sadness he carried with him as he walked up onto the porch and opened the front door. He heard the wagon rumble away and turned to look at it one more time. Firefly stood at the hitchrail, its tail switching, swatting at flies, muscles quivering in its shoulders, which were streaked with fresh blood from insect bites.

Dag entered his house and breathed in the perfume of flowers. He adjusted his eyes to the dim light and saw the vases all around the living room, all of them with morning glories, peonies, black-eyed Susans, honeysuckle, and wisteria.

He walked back to the kitchen and looked at how clean it was, the utensils hanging from the wall near the woodstove, the counters clean, the cupboards washed. *Carmelita*, he thought. Then he forced himself to walk to the bedroom. The empty bed was neatly made and there were cut flowers lying gracefully on the pillows. Laura's dresses hung in the wardrobe and her baubles were on the highboy dresser as if she would return at any moment and slip on a bracelet or a necklace and turn to him for his approval. He looked into the smoky mirror and saw his shadow there, a ghostly visage of a man he hardly knew anymore. His face was gaunt and peppered with tiny bristles, eyes without expression, hat caked with dust and sweat.

He sat down on the bed, hung his head, and lifted his hands to cover his face.

"Oh, Laura," he whispered and then began to weep.

Dag paid off Deutsch a month later and took possession of his mortgage papers, much to Deutsch's displeasure.

"I am sorry about your wife, Dagstaff," Deuce said when Dag got up to leave.

"Deuce, if you ever mention my wife again, I'll kill you, hear?"

"I hear. It was not my fault."

"You're going to prison at Huntsville, Deuce, damn your hide."

"What is this you say?"

"I've got proof that you hired Don Horton to murder me and I'm taking the evidence to the Texas Rangers up in San Antonio."

"You lie, Dagstaff."

"Just watch me, Deuce," Dag said and left.

He found out later that Deutsch lost most of his herd trying to cross the Red at flood stage and he didn't get top dollar for what was left of his herd when he got to Sedalia, Missouri.

Three months later, two Texas Rangers rode up to the Rocking D and arrested Deutsch. He was taken to San Antonio and tried before a magistrate.

Dag testified against him and the prosecuting attorney produced the letter of agreement between Horton and Deuce. Cavins and Flagg testified too as corroborating witnesses in the matter of Horton trying to kill Dagstaff and the killer's subsequent death.

Adolph Deutsch was found guilty of attempted murder and sentenced to twenty years in Huntsville Prison. He would never get out alive.

Dag knelt at his wife's grave. She was buried on a little hill in a grave surrounded by a copse of crepe myrtles. There was a small headstone that Carmelita's husband, Jorge Delgado, had made of hard clay with her name engraved before the clay was fired. The legend read: LAURA DAGSTAFF, and underneath, REST IN PEACE.

Simple, Dag thought, *and eloquent.*

He placed some irises on the little mound of dirt, flowers grown from bulbs Laura had planted shortly after they had married. Fitting. Appropriate.

"Laura," he said, "I was faithful to you, darling. I never strayed none all the time I was gone."

He started to choke up and rose to his feet. He turned to walk back to the house, overcome with grief.

He saw Jo riding up, her hair glistening in the sunlight like the back of a crow's wing.

She lifted a hand and waved to him.

Then he turned back to look at Laura's

grave. He drew a deep breath and turned to meet Jo.

He smiled. *Jo's coming*, he thought. *Now. At this time. Here.*

And then aloud: "I take that as a sign from Laura."

He heard a meadowlark trilling close by, and up on the hill, in the crepe myrtle, a mourning dove cooed a melodious, throaty curdle of deep-throated notes.

He took that as a sign too.